AMISH HONOR

THE AMISH BONNET SISTERS BOOK 2

SAMANTHA PRICE

CHAPTER 1

FLORENCE BAKER WOKE UP EXHAUSTED. She'd just gotten over all the sewing, the organizing, and the cooking for Mercy's wedding, and tomorrow was Honor's birthday. Her throat was dry from breathing the chilly air so she pulled the covers over her head to keep out the cold. Normally when Florence woke, she hurried downstairs to put more logs on the embers from last night's fire and then she'd have a quiet mug of coffee before the rest of the household woke. Today, though, she was weary—weary in body and mind.

Besides doing much of the cooking today for the birthday dinner tomorrow, Florence was determined to come up with a way to make more income in the winter months.

OVER BREAKFAST, Florence asked her family to think hard on what they could do.

"You see, it's important we put money aside for bad seasons. That's why *Dat* had to sell the five acres next door to the Graingers." Florence shook her head. If they still owned that land, and the house that sat on it, they could've had the money from leasing it. The Graingers had since sold to Carter Braithwaite. Florence's father had always hoped to buy back the land, and that was now one of her dreams.

"Any ideas anyone?" *Mamm* asked.

Florence looked at each of her half-sisters, and all of them had blank looks on their faces. All of them, that was, except for Honor.

"I have an idea and, if I can take the buggy, I'll look into it further."

Florence narrowed her eyes at Honor. "Well, what is it?"

HONOR DIDN'T RESPOND. She wasn't only concerned about money for the family. Her idea would also help her to see more of Jonathon Wilkes without anyone looking over her shoulder. The trouble was, Florence didn't like Jonathon, and her youngest sister Cherish had a huge crush on him. Two reasons why she couldn't have him visit at the house.

"What is it, Honor?" *Mamm* finally asked when Honor hadn't answered.

"I'd rather not say until I know if it's a real possibility. All I need is to use the buggy for half a day."

"She just wants to get out of chores," Cherish said.

Joy shook her head at their youngest sister. "That's what you'd do. You can't judge other people like that. In fact, you shouldn't judge people at all."

"You just did."

Joy looked at Favor. "I'd never …"

"You just judged Cherish by saying that's what she'd do."

Florence groaned. "Stop it, all of you. Okay, take one of the buggies, Honor. You can do your chores once you get home."

"Denke, Florence. Of course I will." Honor looked over and saw Cherish staring at her, and Honor knew what she

was thinking. Cherish thought she was sneaking off to spend time with Jonathon Wilkes. She wasn't totally wrong. Her plan did involve Jonathon. If she had a job—say, at the markets—she'd see more of Jonathon with no one knowing.

As soon as Honor arrived at the markets, she headed over to Warren, one of their large customers for apples. He was an *Englischer* who worked with his father in the largest fruit and vegetable stall there.

"Hi, Warren."

"Hello. What are you doing out this way?"

She looked over at Warren's father busy serving some customers. "I'm thinking of looking into having a stall here where we could sell our small goods. We won't sell apples because we don't want to compete with you or our other customers."

"It wouldn't matter if you did," said Warren. "You need to speak with Lionel Pettigrew about getting a stall. He's the manager. I'll put a good word in for you."

"Thank you. That would be appreciated. Where would I find him?"

"I saw him heading out to the parking lot a few minutes ago. I'll see if I can catch him. Stay here."

"Thanks so much."

Warren called out to his father telling him where he was heading. Less than two minutes later, Warren came back with Mr. Pettigrew, a short chubby-cheeked balding man.

Once Warren introduced them, Mr. Pettigrew smiled and said, "Warren tells me that you want to sell apples here."

"No. We have an apple orchard, but we want to sell small goods—canned goods, baked goods=]\ pickles and chutneys here. Also, apple pies and such."

He nodded. "Come with me and I'll show you one or two

spots we might be able to squeeze you in. I'll give you an idea of pricing too."

"Okay, thank you." Before she walked away with the manager, she gave Warren a smile and a nod.

After Mr. Pettigrew had taken her on a tour, showing her where she could set up, he told her the prices. She was pleasantly surprised that they were low in comparison to what she had thought they'd be.

"Is that per week or per month?" she inquired.

"Per month. Is it too much for you?"

"No, not at all."

"And then we have one closer to the front, but that's more than double the size and double the price."

"Would we be able to start with the small one and see how we do?"

"By all means. When would you like to start?"

"We could start tomorrow if that's not too soon."

"That's fine by me. Come with me to my car. I don't have an office at the moment while it's being repainted. I'm reduced to working out of my car. I'll give you some paperwork to sign and bring back tomorrow."

When they got to the car, he pulled some paperwork out of a well-worn leather briefcase and scribbled some figures on it. "Here it is. Read through it and if you agree, bring this with you and be here tomorrow. On the last page, you'll see where to make the weekly payment."

She stared at it to see he'd written a figure even lower than he'd quoted her. "Are you sure?"

"Yes."

"Do we pay at the start of the week or the end?"

"At the start."

"Oh." She wondered what *Mamm* would say about that. "I'll have to get my mother to agree to this first. Don't worry,

I'm sure she will. We run a roadside stand in the warmer months, but it makes so much more sense to be here."

He smiled. "The end of the week is fine if that'll make your mother happier. We all have to keep our mothers happy." He pulled more sheets of paper out of his briefcase. "This is a list of rules." He chuckled. "It's nothing too strange. Operating hours and what not."

She nodded.

"Is it a deal? Assuming your mother agrees?" He put out his hand and she shook it.

"It's a deal." She felt grown-up making a big decision like this with a proper businessman. Now, she just had to get Florence and *Mamm* to agree. Her idea wasn't a new one. Florence had wanted to do it before but *Mamm* had squashed the idea. *Mamm's* main objection had been the cost. Setting up on the roadside was free. In spite of how much a stall was to lease, Honor reckoned they'd make more money there than sitting at home not selling anything. In the springtime they'd have to decide about the roadside stand.

As she traveled toward home, she knew Florence would be okay with the idea and she'd help *Mamm* see it was a good one. The girls could all take it in turns, just like they did with the roadside stand, while Florence stayed home and ran the orchard business.

To put her mother in a good mood, she stopped at their favorite coffee shop and bought her a fancy take out coffee. *Mamm* liked hers with hazelnut-flavored syrup and plenty of chocolate sprinkles. For Florence, she got an oversized chocolate marshmallow cookie to satisfy her sweet tooth.

When she arrived home, Florence was waiting for her on the porch, with her arms folded and looking none too happy.

As soon as Honor stopped the buggy, Florence strode out to meet her.

"You've been gone plenty long enough, and your chores are still waiting."

"*Jah,* I know, but it's my birthday tomorrow and I thought you'd be able to do without me for a little bit. I did something." She stepped down from the buggy. "I committed us to taking out a stall at the markets. I negotiated that we pay at the end of every week and it's not really that much money."

"What markets?"

"The main one in town."

Florence gasped. "The farmers market?"

Honor nodded.

"How much is that going to cost? You didn't sign anything, did you?"

"Not yet. I'll show you." From the passenger side of the buggy, she grabbed the agreement and showed her the figures Mr. Pettigrew had written in.

Florence took the paper and held it up. "That's a lot less than I thought it'd be. Are you sure it's right?"

"*Jah.* I asked him the same question. He wrote it in himself. What do you think?"

Florence narrowed her eyes at her. "You had this idea all by yourself?"

"*Jah,* because we can't stand by the roadside freezing, and what else are we going to do when it's so cold? And how will we make money?"

"We'll get by."

"Yeah, well ... now we can get by better—hopefully. What do you think? Also, we didn't have to commit to a lengthy lease or anything. If we want to stop, we just give one week's notice. It says so right there." She pointed at the rules paperwork that she'd skimmed through on the way home.

Florence wiped away a tear. "You've lightened my load. If

I didn't have so much to think about I would've thought of this."

"I remembered you wanted to do it a couple of years ago."

"Jah, but *Mamm* didn't like the idea."

"Will she allow us to do it now?"

Florence smiled. "You said you've committed us to it."

Honor giggled. "I did. Oh, wait, did I? I don't think so. We shook hands, but nothing is signed."

"Let's unhitch Morgan and then we can tell her together."

"Okay."

"When do we start?" Florence asked.

"He said we can start tomorrow."

"Wunderbaar."

"I got *Mamm* a hazelnut coffee and I got you a great big cookie."

"Ach, denke. I love those giant cookies and the coffee will make *Mamm* happy. Good idea—let's go tell her now."

WHEN THEY WALKED into the kitchen, the girls were all there. They heard what Honor had done while she told their mother. "What do you think, *Mamm?"*

"It's up to Florence. Do you think it's a good idea?"

Florence couldn't hold back her enthusiasm. "I think it's a *wunderbaar* idea. We don't have much to lose and we have enough goods to sell."

Joy nodded. "We do now, but what if we sell out?"

"Then we'll make more," Favor said. "Like we always do, even if we have to stay up into the night."

"Ach nee! The nights are too cold to stay up," said Cherish. "I'd much rather be warm and toasty in bed."

"Honor, why don't you make up a schedule for the girls for the first couple of weeks and also figure out what stock we've got and how long you think it'll last?"

"Okay."

"Can I help?" Hope asked. "I'll get the pens and paper."

"Sure."

"You don't want to work on your birthday, do you, Honor?" *Mamm* asked. "Make sure not to put yourself down to work on your birthday."

"I don't mind."

"Before you do your schedule, stay still for one moment and let's talk about your birthday," *Mamm* said.

"I don't want a fuss. A dinner is fine and I don't want presents."

"Ach, you're easily pleased," said Cherish. "I like loads of presents. Don't tell people you don't want gifts and you can give 'em all to me." Cherish giggled.

"I'd just like a dinner like I always have, but with a couple more people invited. Jonathon, and Isaac too, since they're both staying with Mark and Christina. It would be rude not to include him."

"Jonathon's coming already," Cherish chimed in. When everyone stared at her, she said, "He's our *bruder*-in-law now that Mercy's married Stephen, and he's also staying with Mark and Christina. Mercy might've even married him if she'd met him first. Anyway, I happen to have overheard *Mamm* inviting the four of them."

Mamm nodded. "I did. And there's Ada and Samuel, who'll come too."

Mamm's best friend Ada and her husband were just like family and came to all the girls' birthday dinners.

Florence asked, "Anyone else you'd like to include, Honor, since it's your birthday? Any friends?"

"I'll see my friends through the day, if I'm not going to be working at the market stall. I'll take the buggy and go see them. No need to invite them for dinner. So, just those four will be fine."

"Six." *Mamm* corrected her.

"I meant six. *Gut.*" Honor nodded.

ONCE ALL THE girls had left the kitchen, Florence had a quiet moment alone with *Mamm.* "It's not a good idea for Jonathon to come to Honor's birthday. He should be keeping away from Cherish. You know she's got a crush on him and also I think that Honor likes him."

Mamm shook her head. "We can't leave him out. Besides, I already invited him. He's your *bruder*-in-law now."

"Not really. I don't believe he'd be technically classed as my in-law. He's Mercy's *bruder*-in-law, but he's not mine."

"Besides that, Christina and Mark are coming as well as Isaac, and Jonathon is living on the same property. It would be rude to leave him out."

Florence wasn't happy to hear that. "I'm just trying to stop problems before they start."

"Florence, you're just like your *vadder*—overly cautious."

"Well .... That's a good way to be."

"Not if it's going to upset people and ruin Honor's birthday. Jonathon's coming to Honor's birthday and that's final."

She stared into *Mamm's* eyes. Once her stepmother had made up her mind it was always final. It was rare for her to be firm like she'd been just now, so Florence chose to go along with it. "Okay, but I'm wary of him."

"Why ever for?"

Mamm had never learned how Jonathon had tried to drive a wedge between Mercy and Stephen. Florence had chosen to keep that quiet. She wasn't sure why. "Never mind." It was too long a story to tell and now that Mercy and Stephen were married, *Mamm* would most likely shrug it off.

CHAPTER 2

HONOR SAT down to breakfast on her birthday, missing her older sister. "My first birthday without Mercy. It won't be the same. Why do people have to die and why do people have to leave?"

"*Jah,* it's so unfair," said Cherish. "I want *Dat* to still be here. I miss him. I was his favorite. Now Earl and Mark have gone too."

"We hardly see them either."

"I was *Dat's* favorite," repeated Cherish.

"He didn't have any favorites," Florence had waited for *Mamm* to say that, but since she hadn't, Florence had to stop the back and forth that was inevitable.

Joy said, "Everyone dies. Life's a cycle. We live, and then we grow old and die. Just as the apple tree blossoms, then the blossoms die and the fruit grows, then the fruit shrivels up and it dies too."

Hope screwed up her face. "I don't like the sound of that."

"Yeah, how long did it take you to think of that sad story, *Joy?"* Cherish asked with a scowl.

"I'm just simplifying it for all of you."

"We're not dumb," Cherish said. "You think you know everything."

Joy wrinkled her nose. "I do. I know more than you because I read more."

"Hope and Joy, you're on the stall today, *jah?"*

"That's right. We're going as soon as we finish eating," Hope said.

"Good, some peace today," said Cherish, who didn't get along at all well with Joy.

Thankfully, Joy ignored her as she finished the last of her scrambled egg.

HONOR HAD a day off from the markets since it was her birthday. She helped her *Mamm* in the kitchen while Hope and Joy went to work the market stall and the rest of her sisters cleaned the house.

HONOR WAS happy with herself that she'd made Florence so pleased about opening the stall at the markets. It was the sensible thing to do, she'd been sure, and now everyone could see it. She was even happier that Jonathon was coming to her birthday dinner. She'd helped her mother with the main meal and watched how her mother had made her favorite German dark-chocolate cherry cake.

Florence and her mother were busy in the kitchen when their guests arrived. Cherish pushed Honor out of the way and opened the door to both Isaac and Jonathon who'd come in one buggy. Honor was disappointed about that because it meant they'd have to go home at the same time. It had been her secret hope that Jonathon might stay longer than everyone else so they could talk. Preferably after her younger sisters had gone upstairs to bed.

"Happy birthday, Honor," Isaac said in his large voice that matched his large frame.

"Denke."

"Jah, happy birthday," Jonathon said ignoring Cherish and pushing forward with a huge basket of pink roses.

"Ah, Jonathon. They're beautiful."

Cherish turned and walked away with Isaac while Honor admired the different shades of pink amongst the roses. "I said no birthday presents."

Jonathon leaned forward and whispered, "Maybe it's not a birthday gift."

She giggled. That meant he had brought her flowers. No one had ever given her flowers. *"Denke.* We better join the others." When they sat down, Honor placed the flowers on the low table to the side of the couch.

"Hope, can you tell *Mamm* our guests have arrived?"

"They haven't yet. Ada and Samuel are coming, aren't they? Also, Christina and Mark?"

"They won't be far behind us," Isaac said.

Honor was annoyed with Hope because she never did what she was told until she had argued about it first. She thought she knew better than everyone else and questioned absolutely everything she was asked to do, but Honor couldn't say anything to her about it now in front of the guests.

"Go on, Hope. Just tell her Jonathon and Isaac are here."

"Say please?"

She rolled her eyes. It wasn't worth an argument. "Please?"

"Fine." Hope flounced into the kitchen.

"Is that what she's like all the time?" Jonathon leaned over and whispered to her.

"You don't know the half of it."

Having overheard them, Isaac said quietly, "I'm glad my sister isn't like that."

Honor wondered what Christina was like to Isaac—or had been when she'd been younger. She wasn't very nice to her and her sisters but her half-brother, Mark, didn't seem to notice. Otherwise, he wouldn't have married her.

When Hope came out of the kitchen there was a knock on the door, so she walked over and pulled it open. Honor hurried over to greet the guests. It *was* her birthday, after all.

Christina and Mark had arrived along with Ada and Samuel. "Happy birthday!" they all said at once. Then Mark handed her a gift wrapped in white paper with a red ribbon. She moved away from the doorway so they could move through.

"Mark, I said no gifts."

He chuckled. "I mustn't have heard that part."

"He insisted," Christina said with a rare smile.

"Do I have to open it now?"

"Isn't it your birthday today?" Mark asked.

"You know it is."

"Open it now, then."

Honor was a little embarrassed to open the gift in front of everybody. She never knew how surprised or delighted to look. And what if she hated it? She wasn't good at lying and being false. That was why she preferred no gifts at all. Besides, she didn't need anything. She sat on the couch and carefully unwrapped the parcel while feeling all eyes on her. The first thing she saw was white fabric. Then she lifted it to reveal a beautifully made prayer *kapp* fashioned from sheer organza. She held it up high. "It's beautiful. It's the most *wunderbaar* thing I've ever seen."

"I'm making them," Christina said. "I'm making ones like that to sell."

"I think you'll do very well, but how do you find the time with the new saddlery store?"

"I'm working in the store now remember?" Jonathon said.

"That's right. So, he's working there to give you more free time, Christina?"

Christina nodded and Mark beamed a smile at his wife. "Christina always likes to keep busy."

"It reminds me of the industrious woman from the Bible," Joy said, and then she quoted the entire passage from Proverbs 31 from memory in German.

Sitting back on the couch, Honor whispered to Jonathon, "Joy likes to remind us what it says in the Bible at least five times a day."

He rolled his eyes while shaking his head.

Honor giggled. It seemed as though they thought the same about things.

"That would be extremely annoying," Jonathon whispered back. "I'm not against hearing what the Word says, not at all, but …"

"I know. I mean, once in a while it would be all right, but it's too much. I don't know why she's like that."

He shrugged his shoulders. "Some people are just like that, I guess."

"I guess so."

Florence and *Mamm* came out from the kitchen to greet the guests and then announced that the birthday dinner was ready.

"Before we eat, I want to show both of you what Christina made for me." Honor showed *Mamm* and Florence the prayer *kapp,* and they loved it, praising Christina's workmanship.

When Honor walked into the dining area, which was off from the kitchen, Favor said, "Surprise! I made everyone paper hats and, everyone *has* to wear them."

The hats were in front of everyone's place setting at the table. Once everyone was seated they placed them on their heads with a fair bit of giggling, including the older folk,

Samuel and Ada, who looked especially funny. The women placed the paper hats over their prayer *kapps.* Honor loved the idea and was pleased her sister had gone to the trouble.

When everyone's silent prayer of thanks for the food had been said, Jonathon asked if he could say a special prayer. *Mamm* nodded telling him he could. He prayed for *Gott's* blessings over the Baker family and especially the birthday girl. Then he hesitated and asked for a safe trip for everyone on their way home when the night was over. Then he ended with, "Amen."

"Amen," Samuel and Mark echoed.

For dinner, they were eating roasted chicken and roasted vegetables, with plenty of gravy and mashed potatoes.

"Mrs. Baker, I heard there's volleyball on tomorrow night at the Yoders' *haus* and I'm hoping you'll allow me to take Honor."

Mamm looked over at Honor and then looked back at Jonathon. "Of course, if she wants to go."

"*Jah,* I do."

"I'll bring her home and take her there. You won't have to do a thing."

"I suppose it'll be all right if you take her there and bring her straight back once it's over."

"I will. You can trust me."

"Does that mean you'll be borrowing our spare buggy again?" Christina asked.

"If that's okay?"

Christina nodded.

"I told you it's yours to use when you want," Mark said.

Honor saw Cherish fidgeting in her chair and knew she was going to ask if she could go to the volleyball too. A short sharp kick under the table and a glare from Honor was enough to stop that from happening.

Joy said, "Let me get something straight in my head.

Jonathon, you're working in Mark's saddlery and living in Mark's barn?"

"That's almost right, Joy," said Mark. "It's not a barn. It's off from the stables and it was originally built as living space for workers. It's quite comfortable."

Without commenting on what Mark said, Joy then looked over at Isaac. "And, Isaac, you're Christina's *bruder,* you have no job and you're living with Mark and Christina inside their small *haus?"*

Christina leaned forward. "It's not that small. It's perfect for us and a guest."

Joy raised her eyebrows. "I heard that it was small."

"Not at all." Christina's lips pressed together firmly.

Joy said, "If we'd ever seen it, we could judge for ourselves."

Samuel gave an embarrassed laugh. "What's big to some is small to others."

"It does the job for the both of us." Mark smiled, then added, "The two of us and one guest. Isaac doesn't plan to be with us forever and then it'll be just the two of us again."

"It's not going to be the two of you for long." Cherish giggled.

"This is not a conversation to have over dinner, girls," Florence said frowning at Cherish and Joy.

"I was just asking," Joy said. "And I was going to ask Isaac and Jonathon why they've both moved here. Is that okay or do I have to be someone other than who I am with my own family?"

"Please be someone else," said Hope. "It'd be a nice change."

Favor sniggered.

The night was going downhill fast and Florence sat there tired and exhausted. She couldn't believe Joy's rudeness, but was too weary to reprimand her. Then she was pleased when

Mamm quickly changed the subject. "We have cake for dessert."

"Jah, it's my favorite," Honor said. "*Mamm* always makes it every birthday."

"What kind is it?" Jonathon asked, his gaze fixed on Honor.

"German Dark-chocolate Cherry Cake."

"I don't think I've ever tried that before."

Ada said, "Wilma makes it so well."

"Jah, she does. I've been meaning to get the recipe from you, Wilma," Christina added.

"I'll write it down for you. It came with my *mudder's* family from the Old Country," said *Mamm,* "so sometimes I have to substitute for ingredients I can't get here."

By now it was obvious to everyone that Honor and Jonathon liked one another and Florence wasn't okay with that. Neither was she okay with Cherish's crush on Jonathon. Cherish was far too young to know she was making a fool of herself. Florence looked at *Mamm* to see if she might've noticed what was going on, but she was busily talking with Ada.

When Christina interrupted them and started talking about her prayer *kapps,* Florence was surprised. Whenever Christina had been there for a meal she'd sat at their dinner table looking glum and hardly saying anything at all.

Florence took hold of her glass, raised it to her lips and took a mouthful of water, observing everyone as though she was an outsider. Christina became even livelier when Ada said she might order a *kapp.*

AFTER DINNER when the guests sat in the living room to wait for coffee and chocolate cake, Honor noticed Jonathon making faces at her. He was trying to tell her something.

Then he nodded to his hand and she saw a slip of paper. He had a note to give her. He stood up and she walked close to him and the note was slipped into her hand without anyone seeing.

She slipped the note down the front of her apron as she went past him and on into the kitchen. She tried to help to prepare the dessert, until she was shooed out of the kitchen because it was her special day.

When they were all seated with coffee and hot teas, Caramel, Cherish's dog, rushed downstairs. He jumped on Isaac, sending his coffee flying all over the rug.

"Bad dog." Cherish grabbed his collar and put him outside.

Isaac stood, stunned, and looked down at the coffee. Florence told him not to worry about it.

"I'm so sorry, Mrs. Baker."

"That's okay. It wasn't your fault."

"Caramel doesn't usually behave like that. He just doesn't like you," Jonathon said to Isaac, and everyone laughed.

"Seems so," Isaac replied with a grin.

"Sorry, Isaac. I've got no idea why he did that. He takes a liking to some people and not others," Cherish said.

Isaac sat down again. "Does that mean he likes me?"

"*Nee,* he doesn't. He likes Jonathon, though." Cherish smiled at Jonathon.

Jonathon said to Cherish, "Are you going to leave him out there all night?"

"*Nee.* I'll get him now and put him back in my room."

Honor was pleased to see that Jonathon liked animals.

IT WASN'T until all the guests left that night that Honor sat in her bedroom along with her gift of pink roses to read Jonathon's note.

Meet me tomorrow night outside your house. I'll be there at midnight. I'll throw three tiny pebbles at your window then you climb out your window onto the tree and I'll be waiting for you. Now destroy this note, my love.

She ripped the note into tiny pieces and placed it in the water under the roses so no one would find it. Then she opened her window and looked out. He knew which bedroom window was hers, because she'd pointed it out at Mercy's wedding. He must've noticed that big tree that grew in front of the window alongside the house. *Jah,* she could easily step onto the tree and climb down. In their younger years, she and her sisters had been expert tree climbers. There was little else to do on summer afternoons in the orchard.

CHAPTER 3

JONATHON LOOKED over at Honor as his horse clip-clopped along the road under the amber glow of the sinking sun.

"Why did you give me that note when you knew you were seeing me tonight?" The question had been bugging her since the previous night.

"I just wanted to pass you a note." He smiled at her and she giggled. "You'll never be bored with me," he said.

"I'm learning that."

"You will meet me tonight, won't you? When everyone's asleep?"

"I'd like that."

"Good."

He settled back into his seat. "Isn't night-time volleyball a crazy thing?"

Honor didn't care two hoots about volleyball. Any excuse would've done to be alone with Jonathon. She'd liked him ever since she met him at the harvest, but she had been too shy to say much to him. Things were different now. "The Yoders have night volleyball quite a bit. We stop as soon as it gets too dark, and then we eat and sit around talking."

"Eating and talking are two of my favorite things to do."

Honor giggled. She stared at Jonathon as he concentrated on the road. Against the backdrop of the golden sun she noticed tiny pinpoints of freckles covering his nose and cheeks. It made him look younger than his twenty-three years. "How are you settling in at Mark and Christina's place?"

"Fine. I don't want to be there forever. I need to make a plan to move out. I was talking to Isaac about moving out with me but he seems quite happy doing what he's doing."

"Living with his sister while you're living in the stable, you mean?"

"It's not the stables exactly."

She giggled. "I know. I was only teasing. We heard all about that at my birthday dinner."

"That's right. It's off from the stable, and it's like my own little apartment."

"It sounds cozy. I'd reckon that Isaac's sorry he didn't get to live there."

He chuckled. "He missed it by a day, along with the job at their saddlery store. They'd already promised it to me before they knew Isaac wanted to move here. That's why I feel bad. I figured if Isaac wanted to move out with me, it'd be cheaper with the two of us and we could get a better place."

"Maybe he'll move out soon. When he gets a job."

"I don't think he's going anywhere. I've got an idea he likes someone, but he won't say who. That's why he moved here. I'm not going home that's for certain. It's going to be too crowded there with Mercy and Stephen. At least I've got somewhere to stay and I can stick around here and be close to you."

When he smiled at her she was so happy it felt like one million tiny butterflies had been set loose inside her chest, and all were flapping their wings hard.

"How was your day at the markets?" he asked.

"It was fine, but we're way down toward the back. I'm going to see if we can be moved forward. That might mean we have to pay extra. I don't know how much. We did make more money than at the roadside stand, though."

"It sounds like it was a good move then. It was your idea, wasn't it?"

"It was, this time around. Florence wanted to do it a while ago, but *Mamm* said no back then. But it just makes sense in the cold weather. It'll also be better in the hotter weather if we get to stay there."

BY NOW, people knew Honor and Jonathon liked each other, and there was also an implied understanding between them. Even though no words had been spoken, they were boyfriend and girlfriend.

When they stopped at the Yoder's house they were surprised there were no buggies out front. "Are we early?" Honor asked.

"A little late if anything."

Brett Yoder opened the front door of his house and slowly walked over to them. "Hi, you two. I didn't think anyone was coming so I called it off."

"I said I was coming," Honor told him.

Brett shrugged his shoulders. "Yeah, well I thought you said you *might* come. I'm sorry."

"No harm done," Jonathon said.

"Stay for dinner? It's not ready yet and *Mamm* will love it if you do."

"*Nee,* we couldn't."

"*Jah,* stay. I'll just tell *Mamm* we've got two more people for dinner. She won't mind, she always cooks plenty."

Honor stepped forward. "*Nee* don't. It's okay. We've got somewhere else we can be since the volleyball's not on."

"Are you sure?"

"Quite sure."

"I'm sorry. Everyone else said it's too cold for volleyball now. I can't see why. Volleyball would warm everyone up."

"The days are shorter." Jonathon looked up into the sky. "I think there's only about half an hour of daylight left."

"I guess so. But we didn't have to do volleyball. I'll have to think of something else we can do in the wintertime."

"*Jah,* think up something else, and we'll come to that. Just let us know."

Brett nodded.

"Bye, Brett." Honor was happy since she realized she could have secret time alone with Jonathon. Everyone at home thought she was at volleyball. They could take their time getting back.

"See ya later." Brett stood there, and lifted his hand in a half-hearted wave.

Jonathon gave him a nod and then Honor walked back to the buggy. Jonathon had to hurry to keep up with her. "What's the rush?"

"I'm trying to get away so his *mudder* doesn't see us and make us stay for dinner. If she knows we're here she'll also tell *Mamm* we didn't stay. Oh, unless ... you're not taking me home right now, are you?"

"Not until I have to."

She smiled as they climbed into the buggy at the same time.

He took hold of the reins and clicked his horse onward. "We'll take the time to have some alone time, the two of us. Is that what you had in mind too?"

She looked at him and nodded. "I'd like nothing more. I

was hoping we'd be able to sneak away from the volleyball anyway." She gave a little giggle.

"It suits me just fine. Where do you want to go?"

"Anywhere, I don't care."

"Where can we go so none of your family will pass us and know we're not at the Yoder's house?"

She directed him down a quiet road and then suggested he pull over to the side. "Now we can be alone to talk."

He looked over at her as he looped the reins over one hand. "Good. What do you want to do in life? Where do you see your life headed?"

"I want to help in the orchard with Florence and *Mamm.*"

"I like it around here too. I've liked it here ever since I first arrived."

"What do you remember about me from when you first arrived?"

He chuckled. "Just that there were a bunch of Baker sisters."

"So, you don't remember me?"

"I do. I just didn't want to say it."

That pleased her even more.

"I must admit I feel awful about the fuss that happened with Mercy and Stephen. I was just having a bit of fun with both of them. I didn't know she'd take it the extra step. It made me look like a real cad."

"I know. I think Florence is still mad. She's been so protective over all of us since *Dat* died, and *Mamm's* gone the other way."

"It must be hard to have a parent die."

"It's so hard. *Dat* wasn't even there to see Mark and Christina get married, the first of his *kinner,* or Mercy, and he won't see any of us get married, either. I find it sad."

"Maybe he can see everything from where he is."

She shrugged her shoulders. "I'd like to know if that's right. I don't think we'll ever know."

Slowly he nodded. "I'll tell you something."

"What is it?"

He ruffled his hair. "I don't know if I should've done it but I had a talk with Mark and told him Isaac could have the job."

"What did he say?"

"He wouldn't hear of it. He said I got the job and he's not going to give the job to Isaac just because he's his *bruder*-in-law."

"That was nice of you."

"Or stupid." He chuckled. "At least I still have a job. It's four days a week but it's still a job. I'm not going anywhere now. Now that I've found you I never want to leave."

CHAPTER 4

LATER THAT NIGHT Jonathon brought Honor home at a reasonable hour to keep *Mamm* and Florence happy. After that, when everyone had gone to bed, Honor sat up waiting for Jonathon. When she heard the three tiny pebbles hit the window, she flew into action.

She pulled on two extra pairs of thick stockings, threw a shawl over her shoulders, and slipped into a coat. Then she opened her window slightly. The chilly night air swept into the room and in that moment she had second thoughts about the adventure looming ahead. Spurred on by the thought of seeing Jonathon, she looked out the window. It was a long way down, but aided by the large tree she knew she could easily make it to the ground.

Jonathon's idea had been for her to step out and hang onto the tree and climb down it. That was something she'd never attempted before. Climbing up trees yes, and then back down, but never before had she stepped onto a tree from a height.

When she opened the window further, she sat on the windowsill and looked around for Jonathon. She couldn't see him anywhere. He had to be there somewhere, keeping out of sight. Once she sat on the window frame, she pulled the window down as much as she could, fearing the wind would whistle under her door and through the house and someone would come to find where the cold air was getting in. Now she sat with the window pulled down on her legs.

She took hold of a branch and slipped her legs out of the house until her feet reached a branch. Once she was out, she slid along closer to the tree trunk. Branch by branch she lowered herself, but when she put her foot on the lowest branch, she heard a cracking sound.

Instantly, she knew she was in trouble. The branch gave way beneath her feet, leaving her hanging by her hands. She looked down at the ground. It was too far to jump, but she had no choice. Then the strength in her arms failed, leaving her crashing to the hard ground below.

Pain shot through her foot. She had twisted it when she'd landed on it. She called out in pain. Her sisters or her mother hearing her cries was the last thing on her mind.

Where was Jonathon? Now she was worried that he hadn't tossed those pebbles on the window. Maybe he wasn't there at all. While she was envisioning herself yelling for help at the top of her lungs and having to tell her family she'd fallen out the window, she heard rustling in the nearby bushes. Was it a bear or a wolf?

"Honor, are you okay?" she heard Jonathon whisper as he rushed toward her.

"Do I look like I'm okay?" she snapped.

"I don't know. I can't see you in the dark."

"I fell out of that darn tree when the last branch snapped, and broke my foot," she hissed.

"For real?"

"Jah. Where were you?"

"I was waiting for you where we arranged to meet."

"Your note said you'd be waiting when I climbed out of the tree. Weren't you watching?"

"I wasn't. I was trying to find a spot where we could talk."

"That doesn't make sense."

He sighed. "I was answering the call of nature if you must know."

"Don't tell me that!"

"Well, you kept asking. Put your arm around my neck."

She reached her arm up and hung onto him. He lifted her up and carried her a distance from the tree and laid her down on soft grass. Then, when she straightened her leg, he took off one shoe.

"It's the other foot," she whispered.

"Sorry." Slowly, he eased off the other shoe while she groaned in pain. Once it was off, he asked, "Can you wiggle your toes?"

"I can, but it hurts."

"I don't think it's broken."

"Is that right?" she snapped. "Since when did you become a doctor?"

"I'm only trying to help you, Honor."

"Well you're not helping. It was your idea to meet at night, so it's all your fault."

"Are you blaming me for you falling out of the tree?"

"Yeah. It was your idea." Honor sobbed and he put his arm around her and patted her back. "What am I going to do now? I can't walk inside because everybody will see me and then they'll know I've been out with you. And I'll be grounded for the rest of my entire life and I won't be allowed out until I'm thirty."

He looked up at the tree. "Yeah, it's pretty high up to your bedroom. You might have to sneak back into the *haus.*"

"I won't even make it up the stairs."

"It won't be as bad as you're saying."

"It will. If only *Dat* was still alive. I hate it here now." She sobbed into her hands. Her whole life had changed since her father died. It wasn't the happy home she'd once had.

"Do you?" he asked.

"Jah, and now I'm going to be stuck here until I'm thirty because of this—because of you."

In the moonlight she saw him smiling at her. "That won't happen. I'll wait for you."

"You will?" She was starting to forgive him a little.

"Of course."

"You'd wait until I was thirty and ignore every other woman in the world?"

"I'd wait forever for you. Forever and a day."

She found herself smiling and then tried to move her foot a little. "Oh, it still hurts."

"Don't move it for a while. Give it a rest. Let's talk to take your mind off it. How was your day?"

"We've talked about today just hours ago."

"Let's pretend this is the first time we've seen each other today."

She was willing to do anything to take her mind off her leg. "Fine. I was looking forward to seeing you all day."

He gave a low chuckle. "Me too. I was looking forward to seeing you. I'm so sorry you hurt your foot. You don't blame me, do you?"

"Jah, I do. If I hadn't been coming out to see you then I wouldn't have broken my foot."

"I said I don't think it's broken."

"I'll listen to your medical opinion when you become a doctor. Right now, you can stop telling me it's not broken when it is. It's obvious."

He was silent for a moment. "I've heard that if you have a broken leg you can't wiggle your toes."

"It might be all right, but I won't be able to get back up that tree. Anyway, it's my foot that's broken and not my leg."

"Let's not keep saying the same things. That gets boring real fast."

"Shh. Keep your voice down."

"You, shh."

"Jonathon Wilkes, don't you ever shush me. I don't like the way you speak to me sometimes. I won't take it."

"I'm sorry. I won't do it again."

"I hate being in pain. I haven't been sick for years. Never even had a cold. I'm sorry for being so mean to you, but I'm thinking of how much trouble I'm going to get into and ..."

"Yeah, I know. Florence already hates me and she'll stop us seeing one another. I know, but I have the answer."

"What?"

"I'll carry you up the tree on my back."

"Don't be stupid."

"There's no other way apart from knocking on the front door and you don't want to do that."

She looked over at the tree and wondered if he could possibly do it. It would take great strength. "What if we both fall?"

"Then I'll have a soft landing."

She slapped him on his shoulder. "I'd rather fall on you. That would be fairer."

"Then you carry me up."

She huffed. "We could give it a try. I'm heavier than I look."

"I doubt it. You'd weigh the same as a feather. Let's do it." He leaned over and scooped her into his arms.

"This isn't going to work!"

"It will. Have a little faith." He smiled and then placed her carefully back down onto her feet. Then he crouched down. "Get on my back and hang on. Don't let go for anything."

"I won't and if you drop me, I'll never talk to you again." She leaned forward and placed her arms around his neck and then he started his climb up the tree.

He made gagging sounds. "You're choking me," he whispered.

"I'm sorry." She eased the grip around his neck.

"Hold onto my shoulders instead."

"Okay."

"No! Hold onto me around my neck but try not to cut off my airway."

"I'll try." She readjusted her arms. "Is that better?"

"Jah." He reached up and grabbed hold of the branch, but then he couldn't get further. "It's no use like this. It'll work if I had something to stand on to get me started."

"There's a chair in the barn. Would that work?"

"Where in the barn?"

"Just to the left as you go in."

"You stay here, I'll fetch it." He leaned over and she put her feet onto the ground and then he carefully lowered her.

"Just don't let anyone see you," she whispered.

"I'll do my best." A couple of minutes later he was back with a chair. "I'll get up first, and then you stand on the chair. Get on my back when I tell you."

"Okay."

He stepped onto the chair. "Come on."

She hobbled over and then with him holding onto the branch with one hand and the other under her arm, he hoisted her onto the chair.

"Now hang on."

She jumped onto his back and he groaned.

"Told you I was heavy."

"Don't let go." Inch by inch he made his way up the tree while she ducked her head around the branches. By the time they got to the top, she was relieved. While he stood on a branch that was level with the window, he pulled up her window and turned around so she could move herself in.

Once she was inside, he slipped through the window after her.

"You can't be in here!" she whispered.

"I need to check on your foot."

She hobbled over to the bed and sat down. "I think it's getting swollen."

He looked at it in the warm glow of the kerosene lamp on her nightstand. "It's not too bad."

"It hurts."

"Go to sleep and it might be better by morning." He pulled back the covers for her and she took off her shawl and, still fully clothed, she got into bed. Then he pulled the covers up over her. He kneeled down beside her bed. "When can I see you again?"

"I don't want to go to the markets tomorrow, but I know Florence will force me. She makes us work when we're sick and she won't care about my foot. I'll have to say I jumped out of bed the wrong way." She sighed, not wanting to lie.

"Will you meet me there at the markets?"

"Won't someone see us together?" she asked.

"I don't care. I have to see you."

"*Jah,* me too," she whispered back. "I'll be working on the stall with one of my sisters."

"Is there one of them you can trust?"

"*Nee,* not one. Mercy would've kept my secret, but she was the only one."

"That's too bad. Keep an eye out for me at the markets, then when you see me tell your sister you have to go to the bathroom. By then I would've come up with a plan for us to meet regularly."

"You sure?"

"*Jah,* I can't not see you."

She whispered, "Me too."

"Gut nacht, my sweet." He leaned down and kissed her softly on her forehead.

"Gut nacht, my love."

He got to the window and once he'd gotten a hold of the tree, he slowly closed her window.

The way he'd taken care of her convinced her Florence was wrong. He was a good person and so patient when she'd been so mean. That was just the kind of man she wanted for a husband. She recalled Mercy saying that when you're in love with someone you just know it's right. That's how she felt about Jonathon. She just knew it was right.

CHAPTER 5

THE NEXT MORNING, no one could get Honor out of bed. She was whining about a sore foot and when she didn't get sympathy over that, it had swiftly traveled from her foot to her head. Now she was complaining of a headache.

Finally, she got out of bed and left for the markets with Favor, complaining all the while about what Florence knew was a fake sore foot, and a fake headache.

Once Favor and Honor left and the remainder of the girls were consumed with baking bread, Florence took the opportunity to sit down to have a restful cup of hot tea with *Mamm.* She liked these quiet moments when she got *Mamm* to herself.

"I'm worried about Honor," *Mamm* said. "She's never sick. She's always been the strong one out of them all."

"She was only pretending to get out of work. It's cold and she wants to stay in bed, that's all. I suppose I don't blame her in a way. It's nice to have a break sometimes. It is surprising because I've always seen Honor as the sensible one."

"I know." *Mamm* slowly nodded. "I wouldn't have thought

she'd be the one who wouldn't want to go. The market stall was all her idea."

"Well, you *have* spoiled her. That's why she thinks she's entitled to stay in. She doesn't realize the value of hard work."

Mamm looked over at Florence. "You think I've spoiled her?"

"Jah." Florence laughed. "I think you spoil them all, but Cherish more so. Possibly because she's the youngest."

"It's only because she was so ill when she was younger and I'm so grateful to have her still here with us."

Before Florence could reply, they heard a horse coming to the house. At first Florence was worried that it was the girls back from the markets, but when the sound got louder, Florence knew it was a buggy rather than a wagon.

Mamm looked out the window. "It's Levi Brunner. Whatever is he doing here?" *Mamm* looked very pleased and then Florence recalled that the two of them had been talking a lot at Mercy's wedding.

Levi was a widower with three older children. Two of them had moved communities to marry and the third one, Bliss, was a friend of Favor and Hope's.

Florence walked to the door with Wilma and when they opened it, they saw Levi with a horse tethered to the back of his buggy.

He walked over to them smiling and took off his hat. After he nodded to Florence, he said to Wilma, "I have a spare horse and I thought with all your *dochders* you might be able to use an extra buggy horse. They could go out more and you wouldn't have to drive them everywhere."

Mamm stepped forward. "You're giving us a horse?"

"Jah. Do you like him?" He pointed to the tall bay horse with long black glossy mane and tail.

"He's beautiful, isn't he Florence?"

"He surely is, but we can't accept something like this Levi. Honestly, we can't."

Levi wasn't offended; he simply chuckled. "I don't see why. He's an extra horse for me and one I don't need. I bought him at an auction on impulse." He looked back at the tall bay horse and then turned and smiled at Wilma. "He was the last horse in the program and I reckon everyone had already bought. I got him and I don't use him. I thought you might be able to use him."

"Jah, I think we could use him. *Denke.* The girls will be pleased."

Florence frowned wondering why a man would want the girls to go out more and, anyway, where would they go? *"Denke,* Levi, that's very kind. We were just having some hot tea. Would you like to join us?"

"Jah, I would. Where shall I put the horse?"

Florence pointed to the front paddock. "There's a gate just near where you stopped your buggy."

He turned around. "I see it. I'll put the horse there."

"Very well." Florence and *Mamm* moved back inside the house.

"Why did you say we'd have the horse?"

"It's a gift and it's rude not to accept a gift."

"Do you believe that story he just told?"

A smile hinted around *Mamm's* lips. "I have no reason not to."

"I think he likes you. He might be thinking of making you his next *fraa."*

Mamm laughed. "Don't be ridiculous, Florence. I'm too old for that now."

Wilma wasn't too old. She was only in her mid-forties and that wasn't old at all. Florence wasn't sure how old Levi was, but she was certain he was somewhere around sixty.

Florence headed to the kitchen to re-boil the kettle and

her sisters were still there, busy with bread making. They'd overheard the whole thing and couldn't stop giggling. Florence told them all to keep the noise down and stay in the kitchen until their visitor left. One thing was for certain, Florence was not going to be polite and leave *Mamm* and Levi alone together.

CHAPTER 6

WHILE THE THREE of them sat down in the living room drinking hot tea, there were many awkward silences. Levi kept glancing sideways at Florence most likely wishing she'd leave so he could be alone with Wilma, but Florence stayed.

"What's the horse's name?" Florence asked.

The man stared at her for a while until he finally answered. "Wilbur."

Florence couldn't help being amused. He'd made up that name right then and it was suspiciously close in sound to Wilma. He had probably come straight from the auction with the horse to give to *Mamm.* And why give Wilma a horse? That was something Florence couldn't figure out. Perhaps because a horse was a costly purchase and he wanted to show Wilma his feelings were real.

Florence looked over at her stepmother as Levi talked. There was no hint on Wilma's facial expressions or in her eyes that she liked Levi as anything more than a friend.

"Wilma, why don't you and I try the horse out now?" Levi smiled hopefully at Wilma.

There it was—a possible reason, albeit a very extravagant one to get *Mamm* alone in a buggy with him.

Wilma was silent for a moment, and then said, "Any other time I would, but Honor isn't feeling too well."

Florence raised her eyebrows. She'd never known Wilma to lie or even exaggerate. It wasn't a lie exactly, but Levi would've definitely got the impression that Honor was upstairs sick in bed.

"Might Florence be able to watch her?"

Mamm shook her head.

Florence helped her out. "I'm not the most tolerant or sympathetic person with the sick. I'm used to trees. If I have a sick tree, I cut off a branch or cut it down altogether. Then I burn—"

Wilma cleared her throat. "We get your point, Florence."

"I'm sorry." Florence had been getting carried away. When Levi nodded and just sat there, Florence felt slightly sorry for him. "I'll be happy to take a ride with you if you'd like, Levi?"

Levi blinked rapidly, and then said, "I just remembered I have an appointment in town. I'm sorry, Florence. It went clean out of my mind."

"That's perfectly all right. What I might do then is take Wilbur out myself. He's fully trained and everything, isn't he?"

"Yeah, he's a *wunderbaar* buggy horse."

"We're so grateful for him. We really appreciate it don't we, *Mamm?*"

Wilma nodded vigorously. "We do appreciate it. *Denke* for thinking of our family, Levi."

Levi stood. "I'm happy to help since my two boys have moved out and it's only me and Bliss at home now. Her cooking's not too good since her *mudder* went home to God when she was small. She hasn't had good training."

Florence tried to stop smiling, certain he was angling for a dinner invite.

Wilma didn't seem to notice. "I'm looking forward to Florence telling me how the horse travels. I'm sure he's a *wunderbaar* horse. *Denke* again, Levi."

They both walked him outside. Then they watched him get into his buggy, turn the horse and buggy around and head back down the driveway.

Florence turned to her stepmother. "He likes you a lot."

"Ach nee!" Wilma giggled covering her mouth with her hand. "Do you think so?"

They walked back into the house. "Why else would he give you a horse? And he wanted to go on a buggy ride with you too. Did you see his face when I suggested I go with him to try out the horse? And *Wilbur?* Do you really think that was the horse's name? He had your name on his mind. Wilbur is so close to Wilma it's not funny. Or maybe it is..."

The girls came out of the kitchen and asked their mother what was going on. Florence knew from their smiling faces they'd overheard the whole thing. Now that Florence's quiet time with her stepmother was ruined, she figured she'd try out the new horse. "I'll go for that drive, *Mamm.*"

"Good idea."

Florence left the house and walked over to the horse with a quarter of an apple in her hand. Wilbur looked over at her as soon as she opened the gate. Then he walked over to her and politely took the apple out of her hand and she took the opportunity to slip a lead around his neck.

He didn't so much as flinch when she put the harness on and he even backed nicely into the buggy.

Pleased about the idea of a nice ride alone, Florence set off. She'd only just gotten out of the driveway when a silver car came toward her, a hand waving out the window.

"What now?" she muttered as she looked in the rear view

mirror and pulled her horse to a stop. When the car got closer, she saw it was Carter from next door.

He stopped his car beside her.

"Is that another car?" This was a sedan, and the only one she'd seen before was the white SUV.

"It's a new one. I got tired of the old one."

She smiled and wondered if he might get bored with people just as easily. Is that why he was alone? Wilbur snorted. "This is a new horse. His name is Wilbur."

"That's a coincidence. That's also the name of my car."

She had to laugh at the ridiculous look on his face. He was making fun of her and she was in a good mood and didn't mind playing along. "That's an unusual name for a car. Do you normally name your cars?"

"Just this one. What do you think of her … I mean him?"

"Beautiful, but I think your last one was a little more practical for the country lifestyle, don't you?"

He smiled and wagged a finger at her. "You and I both know that I'm not very country."

"I knew it, but I didn't …. I wasn't sure if you did."

He chuckled. "Where are you headed?"

"Nowhere, really. I'm just trying out the new horse."

He turned his head and looked at the horse. "You never did see my new bathroom and kitchen."

"I will one day."

"Would you like to? I don't want you to feel I'm forcing you."

"Yes. I'd like to see what it looks like now."

"Don't get too excited. The rest of it's the same as the day I moved in."

She nodded not knowing what else to say. One thing she knew was that she didn't want to spend too much time talking with him, but it was hard not to when he was so friendly.

"What about tomorrow?" he asked.

She gulped not expecting him to set a time. "Tomorrow isn't a good day because— "

"The day after?"

She laughed. "You're getting too far ahead of me. What I was trying to say is that we're busy now with the new stall at the farmers market. We have to keep up the supply of things to sell and I have to help the girls in the kitchen."

He pulled his mouth to one side. "What about your bonnet sisters? Couldn't they do without you? There are enough of them."

She rolled her eyes, hating it when he called them that. "I have to supervise."

"Ah, you have to crack the whip?"

"Basically."

His deep hazel eyes stared at her while his head tilted slightly to the side. "Do you really have to work as hard as you do?"

"It's good to work hard."

"No, it's not. Not if you never have any fun and you're not enjoying life. What's the point of living if every day is dull and the same as the one before?"

"My life's not dull." *It wouldn't matter if it was,* she thought. He didn't understand that she didn't live for this life. This life was like the blink of an eye. She looked around to see if any cars or buggies were coming so she'd have an excuse to drive away. "I'm not enjoying life. I mean… What I meant to say was that I am enjoying life."

"Is that right?"

She smiled. "Yes."

"What do you do for fun?" He held up his hand. "Without telling me anything about your apple trees. Other than the orchard, which you'd probably tell me is fun, what do you do?" He lowered his hand.

"I like to sew."

"And?"

She sighed and thought hard about what she'd do if she had unlimited time all to herself. "When I have time at some point, I'm interested in finding early varieties of apples. Ones that are hundreds of years old. My father was trying to do that before he died."

He rested his arm on the window and stuck his head out further. "Is that so?"

She nodded.

"Is that what you want to do, or you want to do it because your father wanted to?"

"I want to do it for myself."

"Tell me about these apples. I never knew they existed. I thought an apple was just an apple. Other than there are green ones and red ones, I know nothing."

She had hoped her enthusiasm for rare apple varieties would bore him, but he seemed more interested. "They do exist, and there are a handful of growers around now trying to get their hands on these varieties."

"Interesting ... and do these particular apples have names?"

She thought for a moment. It had been a while since she'd read her father's journals. "The Narragansett and the Blake."

"And they're hard to find?"

"They are. My father traveled to his cousin's wedding a few years ago and drove past a Blake apple tree in someone's backyard. They let him take a branch for grafting. They didn't know what it was, but my father knew. I was so excited when he brought it home. He'd been talking about wanting to get one of those trees ever since I can remember."

"There's more to you than I first thought."

She laughed. "I'm not sure if that's a compliment."

"It is, and please take it as one."

Wilbur stomped his hoof on the ground a couple of times while snorting. Florence giggled. "That's my signal to move on."

"Hey, Wilbur, you'll have to cut that out. I wasn't finished talking yet." He revved his car. "Now your Wilbur has given my Wilbur a bad example."

She laughed again. "I might see you outside your house one day and I'll come and look at that new kitchen and bathroom."

"Please do." He gave her a smile then put his hand out the window and patted his car door. "Come on, Wilbur, let's go home." Then without so much as a smile or a backward glance, he drove away.

Laughing once more, she moved her horse onward, happier for having seen him.

CHAPTER 7

MEANWHILE AT THE MARKETS, Honor was excited that Jonathon came to see her. She left Favor there and limped away so her sister wouldn't hear them talk.

"I didn't think you'd be here."

"I said I'd be here." He looked down. "How's your foot?"

"It's okay. It's not broken. It's getting better. I can walk on it."

"Just as well for me or you'd never let me forget it."

She giggled.

"Christina asked me to ask you something."

"What is it?"

"Would you come to their place for dinner?"

Honor was more than a little shocked. "Me?"

He smiled and nodded. "That's right. I'll be there too, of course."

"To dinner?" she squeaked.

He chuckled. "Why are you talking like that?"

"In the whole time she's been married, I've never known her to invite anybody over for dinner. Not even *Mamm.*"

"She's invited you."

"And who else?"

He shrugged his shoulders. "I'm not sure."

"Isaac?"

"Nee, he won't be with us tomorrow night."

"She's invited me for dinner tomorrow night?"

"That's right. And ... what shall I tell her?"

"Tell her yes, of course."

He smiled. "It's another way for us to see each other. I'll collect you, and bring you back to your place when the dinner is over."

"Did you ask her to invite me?"

He shook his head. "She just offered. Maybe because they came to your birthday dinner?"

"Nee. It couldn't be that. They come to all our birthday dinners and she's never felt obligated to repay that in any way."

"Maybe she's got a new recipe she's trying out."

"Or, she might've changed. She was nicer at my birthday than I've ever seen her and she made me that *kapp.* Do you think I should wear it to her place for dinner?"

"That would be a way of showing your appreciation, I reckon."

"Okay." She hoped she hadn't said too much. She was talking as though Christina was a mean person. "I hope you don't think anything bad about Christina. I like her and everything, it's just that the dinner thing is a bit out of character."

"People can change. Look at me."

"What do you mean?"

"I've become a better person because of you. Same with Isaac. He tells me there's someone he likes. I can see him growing softer and growing up a bit."

"You've only known him a week."

"Sometimes that's all it takes," he said with a grin.

"I wonder who he likes?" Honor tapped her chin with her finger.

"I got the feeling it was one of your sisters."

"*Nee,* it couldn't be. He's not been near the *haus* other than at the wedding."

He shrugged his shoulders. "Maybe I'm wrong, but he arrived here for Mercy's wedding and now he's stayed on. Only because he's met someone, that's my guess. What about Joy? She's the next oldest to you, isn't she?"

"It wouldn't be her. I don't think anyone would be good enough for Joy unless they could recite the Bible backwards and forwards and then backwards again."

He chuckled. "We've talked a fair bit and he hasn't offered the information about exactly who he likes, so I was polite enough not to ask."

Honor nodded. "Since you've talked, does Isaac ever tell you what Christina was like when they were growing up?"

"He said they went their separate ways most of the time. She's older and they weren't really that close, but he likes Mark. He said he's been a *gut bruder*-in-law."

"In what way? They didn't even give him a job at the saddlery." She was teasing him and she was glad he didn't take it seriously.

"He would've been a bit disappointed to hear he missed the job by about one day. But it wasn't meant to be and something else will turn up for him. Probably something he's better suited for. I didn't know if I could be confined within four walls of a store all the daylong. I like to be out in the fresh air doing things with my hands, but I've coped well. It's a good job and the business is doing well, so the job's secure."

"I hope so."

Suddenly Honor felt someone pull her arm. She turned to see it was Favor. "I need help back there."

“I’m coming. I was just talking to Jonathon. Go back. I’ll be there in a minute.”

Favor clamped her lips together in a clearly dissatisfied manner, and then turned and walked away.

“I have to go.”

“Yeah, me too,” he said.

They smiled at one another before they went their separate ways.

WHEN HONOR ARRIVED HOME, she told everybody Christina had invited her to dinner—everybody was just as shocked as she’d been.

"Why are you going there for dinner?" Joy asked.

"I'm not sure, but Jonathon told me Christina invited me."

"Us too?" Cherish asked.

"Nee."

"What about me?" Joy asked.

"She just said none of us,” Favor said. "She especially wouldn't want to ask you."

Joy’s mouth fell open. "Stop being so mean."

"Stop it all of you!” *Mamm* said. "You girls will be the death of me one day, the way you argue all the time."

Joy said, "it's not me, it's her." She pointed at Favor. "You should do something about her, *Mamm.* She’s so disrespectful.”

Florence said, “All of you be quiet and that includes you, Joy. You heard *Mamm.”* Florence looked over at Honor. “When are you going for this dinner?"

"Tomorrow night."

"She must want you to marry Jonathon," Hope said with a giggle.

“There's no need to rush into anything, Honor," *Mamm* said.

"I'm not going to get married any time soon, don't worry about that." Honor smiled.

"I didn't know how much I would miss Mercy, and I'm in no hurry to lose any more of you."

"You should've thought of that before you had Stephen to dinner, *Mamm,"* Favor said.

"And had him help with the harvest," added Joy.

Cherish said, "It wasn't *Mamm's* idea, it was Ada's. She said it was planned all along to marry off her nephew."

Florence held her head. All of this chatter was making it ache.

CHAPTER 8

ON FRIDAY, Jonathon brought Honor to Christina and Mark's house for dinner. They stood at the closed front door and smiled at one another for a moment before Jonathon lifted his hand to knock.

The door swung open and Christina smiled immediately. "*Ach,* Honor, you're wearing my prayer *kapp*."

Honor touched the strings of the carefully made *kapp.* "I am and I love it."

Christina grinned. "Be sure to tell everyone where you got it. That'll help me sell a few more."

"Sure, I'll do that. It would be nice to be able to sew as good as you."

"There's no reason why you can't. It's only being shown what to do and then doing it over and over again. Hasn't Florence shown you how?"

"*Jah,* but we've only got one sewing machine and it belongs to Florence. It's one of those treadle ones. It can be converted to use a gas-powered motor, but mostly we don't do that."

"Same as mine. I would offer you to come over here and sew, but I'll be on my machine most of the time."

"Denke anyway."

Christina then smiled and laughed as she stepped aside to allow them through. "Sorry to leave you standing at the door in the cold. I was just so pleased to see you wearing my *kapp,* Honor."

"Well, it's hers now," Jonathon said.

Christina laughed. This was a different Christina from the one Honor knew. She was being extra nice and friendly. Both Christina and Mark got along well with Jonathon, so perhaps he'd told Christina his feelings and she was helping the two of them develop their relationship. Having both Christina and Mark approve of Jonathon reinforced her feelings for him. It made things difficult with Florence being so against him.

Christina sat them down with Mark in the living room.

After they greeted Mark, Jonathon said, "Tell us how you two met."

Mark chuckled and looked over at Christina. "We were both on *rumspringa* when we met. Being from different communities, I didn't even know she was Amish. We returned and got married and she moved here. Then we wanted to open a business together and that's when we heard about the saddlery being for sale."

"Ah, a real romance story," Jonathon said.

"Can I help you with anything in the kitchen?" Honor asked Christina when she stood up.

"Nee, I'm fine. Everything is fine."

Honor sat down next to Mark and the conversation drifted into work.

When there was a pause, Honor asked, "Where is Isaac tonight?"

"We don't see him much anymore. He comes and goes when he pleases. He doesn't need to check in with us."

"I realize that, but I just thought he might have said where he was going." When they both stared at her she realized it sounded like she cared too much where Isaac was. She coughed. "It's just that someone had asked me if he'd be here tonight, that's all."

"Has an admirer, does he?" Mark chuckled.

"Hardly, he's a bit old for that."

"But that doesn't stop one of your sisters having a crush on him," Jonathon pointed out mischievously.

"Dinner is ready now," Christina called out.

They all moved to the kitchen. When they all sat around the cramped table with barely room for four people, Honor realized why they rarely invited people to the house. There was simply no room unless some of the people sat on the couch with their dinner on their laps. Then as Mark sat down, Honor's gaze swept over the food. There was a large dish of something that looked like bologna, and a green salad, potato salad, cooked ham and gravy.

Once all of them were seated, they each bowed their heads and gave a silent prayer of thanks for the food.

When Honor opened her eyes, she looked again at the food. "This all looks so good."

"So long as it tastes good," Christina said. Christina then stood and dished out the food onto everybody's plates.

After that, everyone was quiet for a while as they ate the first couple of mouthfuls. Then Honor thought it was best to compliment Christina on the food, even though it wasn't that great. That's what their dinner guests did at home, but they probably meant it. "Mmm, this is nice, Christina."

"Denke."

"Jah, it is. The wedding went well the other day," Mark said to Honor.

"It did. It was the first one in *Mamm's* house. Since you got married in Christina's community at her parents' *haus."*

"I'd reckon *Mamm's* still talking about that, is she?" Mark asked.

Christina smiled. "She wasn't too happy about that."

"Wasn't she?" Jonathon asked.

Mark shook his head. "I can't say I don't understand. She would've wanted me to get married here. Since we had planned on living here after we were married, I should've got married surrounded by her friends in the community where I was raised. She didn't exactly say that, but that's a round-about way of saying what she thought."

Honor recalled all the fuss at the time. It wasn't long after *Dat* died and *Mamm* insisted it was too far to travel and too much trouble to go to Mark's wedding. Was that why Christina was a little frosty with *Mamm* and acted stand-offish with the rest of the family?

Of course, there were two sides to everything and Honor hadn't heard *Mamm's,* but she wasn't going to ask. "What's it like to have your *bruder* around all the time, Christina?"

"Good. I've really missed him these last couple of years. I still don't see him much because he's out of the house most of the time looking for work."

"Are you missing Mercy?" Mark asked Honor.

"I am. We were always together. Now I'm closest with Hope."

"What about Joy?" Christina asked.

"Joy's a loner. She prefers to stay in her room and read. She reads for hours a day whenever she's not doing chores."

"What does she read? The Bible all the time?"

"Jah. She must've read it through three times by now. If you say a verse she'll tell you where it is in the Bible and sometimes the exact chapter and verse."

"Isn't that a good thing?" Christina asked.

"*Jah,* I'm not saying it's bad. Of course, it's good." Honor looked down at her food and then she looked up at everybody. Jonathon was smiling at her and she knew they both thought Joy was annoying. They could communicate without the exchange of words.

CHAPTER 9

THREE HOURS LATER, after dinner and two cups of coffee, Honor was delighted to climb into Jonathon's buggy to be taken home.

When Jonathon sat next to her, he whispered, "I thought the night would never end."

"Me too."

He chuckled and moved the horse forward. "I didn't know there was so much to do with prayer *kapps."* He shook his head. Christina had spent a lot of time talking about them. "Are there different designs or something? I've never noticed."

"There are different ways of making them. Just ask your *schweschder,* she'll tell you."

"Nee denke. And I have no *schweschder* to ask. Plus I've heard more than enough about them to last me a lifetime. I already know more about them than most men know. Except for Mark."

THEY BOTH LAUGHED as he turned the buggy onto the road.

"Honor, what do you think your family would think about us marrying?"

"They'd say I'm too young. Far too young and now with Mercy having moved away, *Mamm* misses her. They'll be against it."

"That's hard. I'd marry you tomorrow if you were older."

"Would you?"

He looked over at her. "For sure."

"We'll have to wait."

He sighed. "I've never been good at waiting."

"Me neither."

"Meet me tomorrow at the markets? I'll try to get there to see you as soon as I can get away from work. Sometimes Mark sends me on errands."

"Sure. I'll keep a look-out for you.

FLORENCE STARED out the window when Jonathon brought Honor home. Everyone else had gone to bed and it had been up to her to wait up. She pulled the curtain aside and waited while tapping her foot on the floorboards. It was too dark to see inside the buggy.

After a couple of minutes, Honor still hadn't gotten out of the buggy and Florence was seeing red. She stomped to the front door, swung it wide open not caring the least about the cold air that would whistle into the house, and she got to the buggy door just as Honor was getting out.

"Get to the *haus!"* Florence hissed.

"What's the matter with you?"

Through gritted teeth, she said, "Just do it."

Honor hurried into the house and then Jonathon said, "Good evening, Florence."

Florence glanced over her shoulder to see Honor inside

and then she turned back to Jonathon. "Why don't you leave her alone and find someone more like yourself?"

He frowned at her. "I want to marry Honor. It's a matter of timing."

Florence recoiled. "You can say that again. 'Timing' is right though, because there's no time in this world that I'll ever allow you to marry Honor. I'll tell her that trick you played on Mercy."

"She knows all about it. We tell each other everything."

"I'm sure the way you tell it and the way I will tell it will be vastly different. Jonathon, why don't you go back home?"

He stared at her looking hurt and Florence turned her back on him and stomped back to the *haus.*

As soon as Florence got into the *haus,* Honor was standing there. "What did you say to him?"

"I told him how things would be from now on."

"Why do you care so much about him? You're acting like he's horrible and he's not. He's a decent person. Even Mark and Christina like him. Doesn't that say something? Your own *bruder* has him working in his business."

"Having him working and having him marry someone close to you are two very different things."

Honor shook her head. "I'm going to bed. Can we talk about this another time?"

"*Jah,* tomorrow."

"I'm going to the markets early. Can we talk when I get home?"

Florence nodded. "Sure." Honor walked upstairs and Florence was pleased that Honor was taking everything so well. She'd expected a big argument.

CHAPTER 10

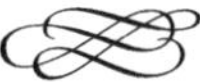

THE NEXT DAY, Honor went to the markets, taking her turn with Joy.

The first customers of the day had only begun to wander through the markets when Honor looked up from straightening the stock and saw Jonathon. She told Joy she needed to go to the bathroom.

She headed off in the direction of the ladies room and then with a quick look over her shoulder to make sure Joy wasn't looking, she took a detour toward Jonathon. She met with Jonathon behind a stall displaying tall hanging rugs.

"You're early," was the first thing she said. "Now I've got nothing to look forward to for the rest of the day except finishing time."

He touched her shoulder lightly and then his fingers traveled down her arm to take hold of her hand. "I couldn't wait another minute to see you."

"How did you get out of work? Did Mark have an errand for you?"

"I told Mark I needed to post an urgent letter, so I don't have long. I'll have to get back."

"I have to be quick too. I'm sorry about Florence last night. She's so protective she's ridiculous sometimes."

"You've got nothing to be sorry about. Her being against us is going to make things even harder for us."

Honor rolled her eyes. "Don't say that."

"I've been thinking. I've got an idea, but it'll be a big risk."

"What is it?"

"What if we run away together?"

She gasped. "Could we do that?"

"I don't see why not. The way Florence spoke to me last night, I don't see we have any other choice."

Honor was upset at Florence interfering, acting like her mother. "Where would we go?"

Jonathon looked around. "Back home. I know some people about ten miles from my folks' home and I reckon I could find a job with them pretty easy. I had a job lined up, but I threw it in when I moved here. If I don't get a job there I've got other ideas."

"Doing what?"

"It doesn't matter what I'm doing. As long as we can stay together I'd get a job doing anything."

"We can't get married until I'm eighteen." She sighed. "It's no use."

"We can be together until we marry. I'd rent us a place. We'd have to pretend to be *Englischers* and once we're married, we can go back to the community. Maybe a community where no one knows us. We can get baptized and be proper members and all that."

"I'd rather it not be like that."

"I know, I'd rather a lot of things, but sometimes life doesn't work out how we'd like it and we have to work out other ways around things." He moved some strands of hair away from her forehead. "Don't pout."

"I'm not pouting."

His eyebrows drew together. "Until we're married we'd have two rooms of course, if that's what you're worried about. If we can only afford a one bedroom place I'll sleep on the couch."

"Do you mean it?"

"Jah. Everyone thinks I'm a bad person and I have done some pretty rotten things, but I don't want to be like that anymore. I've changed since I've met you."

She giggled. "Can I trust you?"

"Can I trust you?" he asked sporting a crooked smile.

"Jah. I want everything to be proper."

"I can live with that. It won't be proper in one way, but I get where you're coming from."

"Okay let's do it."

"What, run away?"

"Jah."

A smile beamed across his face. "Do you mean it?"

She giggled. "I do." She stepped out from behind one of the rugs on a stand and saw her sister back at the stall serving two people at once. "I better get back to work and help Joy."

"Can you arrange to come here tomorrow as well? I could meet you at lunchtime and by then I'll have our escape plan figured out."

"Sure. Wait. Tomorrow is Sunday and the meeting is on at the Fishers' *haus."*

He chuckled. "So it is. I'll see you there and we'll have to find each other during the meal."

"Okay."

He smiled and gave her a nod. "I should go."

"Okay." She turned and hurried back to help her sister. What they were planning was wrong, but she couldn't see any other way."

"Where have you been?" Joy asked when the customers were gone.

"I wasn't sure where the toilets were."

Joy frowned at her. "You've been to them before."

"I found them eventually."

"Don't take that long again. I was swamped with customers."

"You must've sold a lot then."

"I did. But sometimes people don't want to wait to be served, and they just leave. We need to sell as much as we can to keep Florence happy."

"All right. I'm sorry." Honor shrugged her shoulders.

THE NEXT DAY, Honor briefly saw Jonathon after the meeting. There was a family visiting from another community, so people were preoccupied with them. That left Honor and Jonathon to talk unnoticed.

"I've booked us tickets. At five in the morning, meet me outside your place on the corner. I'll be in a taxi waiting."

"Tomorrow morning?"

"*Jah.* Only bring a small bag of things with you. I'm bringing one bag, and I already bought some *Englisch* clothes for you, so I'll bring them with me. Write a letter and leave it in your room telling everyone you've gone somewhere and not to worry. Otherwise, they'll think you've been kidnapped."

"*Jah,* okay, and what time did you say?"

"Five in the morning and, what did I say for you to bring? Repeat it so I'll know you'll remember."

She giggled. "I'm not to bring much, and you said you'll bring clothes for me."

"And?"

"Write a letter so they don't think I've been kidnapped."

"Good. I'll see you tomorrow and whatever you do, don't be late or we'll miss the bus."

"Got it."

"You won't change your mind, will you?"

She shook her head. "Never."

He looked around and then said, "We'll be a long way from your home, and I mean a long way."

"I don't care as long as I'm with you."

They exchanged smiles and went their separate ways.

CHAPTER 11

THE NEXT MORNING, Florence was making breakfast when Favor rushed into the room. *"Mamm,* Hope and I can't find Honor anywhere and she's not in her room."

Mamm, who was sitting at the breakfast table, put down her mug of coffee. "Well she'd better hurry or you'll be late for the markets."

Joy walked into the kitchen. "She didn't want to go the other day, and now she's pulled this stunt to get out of it."

"She wouldn't do that," *Mamm* said. "She was the one who wanted us to have the stall."

Hope held her hands in the air. "She's nowhere in the *haus* —we've looked everywhere."

"I'll help you look outside," Joy said. "Maybe she's helping in the barn getting the wagon ready."

"Nee," Hope said. "She'd wait for me to help her do it."

"I'll help," Florence said. "Everyone, look for Honor."

All the girls left what they were doing and searched through the house, and then went outside, through the gardens, calling out everywhere.

"Is she in the orchard?" Favor asked.

"Could be," Florence said, "We'll have to split up and have a look."

The girls went through the orchard hollering for Honor at the top of their lungs, but still there was no reply.

"I don't know what to do," said Favor. "We should be leaving right now. "

"Joy, you go with Favor today. I'll take the buggy and go looking for her."

"I should stay with *Mamm* and Hope should stay too. Cherish and Favor can go to the markets. They're quite capable of going on their own."

Florence shook her head. "They aren't old enough."

"I'll drive them there and back. I really think I should be here with *Mamm.*"

"Okay."

"She's done this deliberately to get out of it," Cherish grumbled.

"*Nee,* she's not getting out of anything. She'll be punished with extra chores. She'll be every day at the markets for the next two weeks running." Florence was worried because Honor was usually the sensible one.

Joy rolled her eyes. "We'll take the buggy."

"Okay, but hurry," Florence urged.

While Favor and Cherish were outside hitching the buggy, Joy sat on the couch giving Caramel a final pat. "I'm going to look for Honor after I take the girls to the markets, *Mamm.*"

Mamm was now sitting on the couch next to Hope, and she looked up at her. "Where will you go?"

"I don't know."

"I'll come too," said Hope bounding to her feet.

"Nee, you stay with *Mamm."* She hurried out the door and

then heard the front door open and looked over her shoulder to see Hope hurrying after her. She stopped until Hope caught up.

"I want to come too."

"You can't. Can't you see how upset *Mamm* is?"

"She's okay."

"Nee she's distraught, or will be as soon as she realizes Honor hasn't gone for a walk."

"Okay. I'll stay. Where are you going?"

"I'm stopping by all her friends' places." She wasn't, but she couldn't tell Hope she was going to see Isaac.

"Okay."

"Go back inside and sit with *Mamm."*

"I'm going."

ONCE CHERISH and Favor left with Joy, Florence had another look through the house. Honor knew that when one girl stopped working it put pressure on all the others. That's why it was surprising that she would go somewhere without telling anyone.

She walked upstairs and, once more, looked in all the bedrooms, under everybody's beds, and then in all the closets. Then she had an idea—the attic. She lit a lantern and climbed up into the attic. She held out the lantern to light all the corners and there was no Honor. The attic was where her late mother's possessions were boxed. One day when she had time, she'd go through them again and be reminded of what was there. It would have to be when everyone was out and that was something that hardly ever happened.

Now, she was starting to get seriously worried about Honor. She went back to the kitchen to see how Wilma was doing.

"Have you found her?" *Mamm* asked.

"Nee. When did you last see her?"

"Last night. She'll turn up. I finished making the breakfast," *Mamm* said.

Florence had clean forgotten the breakfast she'd been making. The girls had also gone to the markets with no breakfast. Honor had a lot to answer for when she got back. Florence looked down at the eggs and bacon. *"Denke, Mamm."* She sat down to eat. "Are you eating?"

"We already had something while you were in the attic."

Her mother didn't seem too concerned, or if she was, she was covering it up pretty well.

Mamm's calmness helped to soothe Florence a little, and thinking she might need her strength later, she ate breakfast.

When breakfast was finished and Honor still hadn't shown up, Florence announced she was going to hitch the buggy and go out looking.

"Okay. I thought she'd come home once it was too late to leave for the markets. She didn't." Now, *Mamm* was starting to worry.

"I'm sure she won't be far. You know what? She's probably out visiting someone."

"Who would she possibly be visiting at the crack of dawn?"

"Do you want me to come with you?" Hope asked.

"Nee, I'll go alone. You stay home with *Mamm,* and when Honor shows up, tell her how much trouble she'll be in when I get back."

"Gladly." Hope giggled.

She led Wilbur out of his stall that was connected to his paddock. He looked a little dismayed that she'd brought no tasty morsel with her today. "I'm sorry, boy, but this is an emergency." She patted his neck. "I'll give you an apple when we get back—a whole one."

A dark gloominess weighed upon Florence as a heavy feeling of foreboding settled in. She tried not to let bad thoughts gnaw at her tummy and cloud her judgment. While she hitched the buggy, she planned her search. There was no wavering in her mind over where her first stop was. She had to make sure Jonathon was where he was supposed to be.

CHAPTER 12

MARK AND CHRISTINA's house was closer than the saddlery store where Jonathon worked, so Florence stopped there first. She jumped out of the buggy and knocked on the door. As soon as Christina opened it, Florence blurted out, "Do you know where Jonathon is? Is he here?"

Christina lifted up her chin in a surprised manner. "He's gone."

"What do you mean, 'he's gone?'" Florence's throat constricted and she could hardly say the words.

"He was supposed to travel to the store with Mark today. He didn't meet Mark at the buggy so he went to Jonathon's room and he wasn't there. All his stuff has gone too. He left without saying anything."

Florence sank to the cold boards of the porch while Christina kept talking.

"He was supposed to work today because Mark and I had somewhere important we were supposed to be and he was going to be the only one in the store. He let us down badly." Then Christina repeated, "He's not in his room and all his stuff is gone,"

Florence's hand flew to her neck. "Really?"

"You can have a look if you don't believe me."

"I do believe you. I just cannot believe this is happening."

Christina scratched her face. "Why are you here so early in the day? And why are you asking about Jonathon?"

Florence gulped not knowing how much she could say to Christina. If Jonathon and Honor weren't somewhere together, she didn't want Christina knowing that she thought they might be. "I just wanted to know if he could help with something in the orchard."

"*Nee* he can't because he's not here. I'm sorry that Mercy brought him into the family. It's all her fault."

"How's it Mercy's fault?"

"She married Stephen and if she hadn't married Stephen we wouldn't have let Jonathon stay here."

"That's a bit far-fetched to blame Mercy." Florence gathered her strength. She was going to need it.

"It makes sense."

"Anyway, I've got to go. If Jonathon can't help me I need to find someone who can."

Christina eyed her suspiciously. "What did you want him to do?"

"I've got to go."

"*Nee,* wait."

"I'm in a hurry." She climbed into her buggy before her sister-in-law interrogated her further.

Driving away, she was sick to the very pit of her stomach.

Both of them have gone missing.

There was a good chance they'd run away together and Honor wasn't yet eighteen, not for almost an entire year.

FLORENCE HAD no idea what she was going to do next. She headed toward home, but she couldn't tell her stepmother that her daughter had run away with a man in his early twenties. Her mother would surely have a heart attack. And right now, Florence almost felt like she was going to have one. The only thing she could do was find them.

They'd be trying to get out of town.

If they'd run away together they wouldn't stay close by. She drove on into town, passing the local bus stops and hoping to see them, but there was no sign.

It was too much—too much for her to handle on her own. She had to tell her stepmother and together they'd decide what to do next. Her stomach was doing summersaults all the way home.

Just as she was about to turn the buggy into her driveway, she noticed Carter's car on the road coming in her direction.

He has a car!

She stopped her horse, jumped out of the buggy and waved him down. The car would be much faster than a buggy and this was an emergency.

He stopped his car, rolled down his window, and then she hurried over to him. "What are you doing right now for the next few hours?"

"Nothing that can't wait. Why, what's wrong?"

"I'll tell you on the way. Follow me up the driveway, and I'll leave the horse and buggy at home."

"Okay."

She got back into the buggy, and as she said a quick prayer of thanks she headed up the driveway while changing her plans. A minute later, she burst into the kitchen. "*Mamm*, get Hope to unhitch the buggy. I've got something I need to do."

"Is everything alright?"

"Did you find her?" Hope asked.

"*Nee.* Don't forget the buggy. I've got to go."

"I'll do it for you," Hope called out after her as she walked outside.

"Denke." Florence got into the car and as Carter drove away, she looked back and saw both Hope and her stepmother at the front door staring after her.

"They've never seen you in a car before?"

"It's not that. We do travel in cars, we just don't drive them. I didn't tell them where I was going or what I was doing. Or who I was going with."

"You haven't told me where we're going either."

She took a deep breath and tried to calm herself. "My little sister is missing and so is the boy she likes. He's not a boy, he's a man and she's only seventeen."

"Back up a minute. Are you saying that they're together?" He glanced over at her.

"That's my fear." She nibbled on the end of a fingernail.

"That's not good."

"I know that."

"Where are we going?"

"I figure they're trying to get away, so train stations, bus stations, everywhere ... or anywhere they might've gone."

"Hotels?" he asked as he moved the car onto the road.

She frowned at him. "What do you mean, 'hotels?'"

He raised his eyebrows.

"Oh, don't even say that; don't even think that."

"Surely that's what you're thinking?"

"No! My sister's not like that." She gulped when she realized her sister was with a man who probably would try to take every advantage he could. She'd never liked Jonathon and now she was being proved right.

"She's only human. These things happen. You hear about them all the time."

They were wasting time talking. All she wanted to do was

get going. “Not my sister. Anyway, we can’t knock on all the hotel doors in the county.”

"Do you think you should call the police? I mean she’s seventeen. I don’t know, but isn’t that kidnapping?"

“She would’ve gone willingly.” She knew her stepmother would hate the idea of getting outsiders involved. That’s why she had to find Honor—and fast. "Maybe, I don't know. Let's just try to find them first.”

"Sure.” He pushed some buttons on the dashboard of his vehicle. “This will tell us where all the bus stops and train stations are.”

"Really?"

He nodded. "It's called technology.”

She remained silent.

CHAPTER 13

ONCE JOY HELPED Favor and Cherish set up the stall, she headed back to the buggy wondering where Honor might be. In her heart, she knew she was somewhere with Jonathon. Her first stop would have to be Christina and Mark's house since Jonathon was staying on their property.

If Honor wasn't with Jonathon, then Jonathon would be at work. Rather than raise alarm bells, she hoped Isaac knew something. Jonathon might've confided in him since they both lived on the same property.

When Joy stopped the buggy outside Mark and Christina's house, she hoped Christina would be out. She knocked on the door hoping to see Isaac standing there, but when the door opened it was Christina.

"Joy!" Christina looked over Joy's shoulder.

"I'm here by myself," Joy told her.

"Come in."

Joy walked through the doorway and then Christina turned around to face her.

"Is Isaac here?"

Christina raised an eyebrow. "Florence was just here

looking for Jonathon and now you're looking for Isaac. What's going on?"

"Florence was here looking for Jonathon?"

"Jah."

"And, where is he?"

"He's gone. He's left without a word. He was supposed to work today, but Mark had to work. Tell me, what is going on? I know something is."

Joy drew in a deep breath. "Don't say anything to anyone, but Honor is missing and ... and I am thinking she might've gone somewhere with Jonathon."

Christina frowned. "Where?"

"I don't know. Do you know where Isaac might be?"

"He's at a job interview. It should be finished by now."

"Do you know where?"

"At the timber mill. The one down by Old Mill Creek Road."

"I'll see if I can find him and ask him if he knows anything."

"Good idea. You said Honor has gone too?"

"Jah."

"It figures. Jonathon has always struck me as someone who's unreliable. I told Mark, but he saw something in him that I couldn't see. Now this has happened. That'll teach Mark to listen to me."

"I'll have to keep looking for Honor."

"I'll pray you find her quickly."

"Denke."

She hurried out of Mark and Christina's house, got back in the buggy and turned the horse toward Old Mill Creek Road. Just when she was nearly at the timber mill, she was relieved to see Isaac's buggy on the road coming toward her.

He slowed down when she got closer, and then he pulled his buggy over to one side.

He jumped down from the buggy and hurried over to her. When he saw her face, he asked, "What is it?"

She stepped down from her buggy. "It's Honor. She's missing."

"Since when?"

"She was supposed to go to the markets today and when I went to wake her up she wasn't there. She's run away from home."

"Are you sure?"

She nodded. "Jonathon's missing too and she has a huge crush on him. She thinks she's in love with him."

"You think she ran away with Jonathon?"

"Jah!" She repeated, "She has a giant crush on him."

He shook his head and looked at the ground.

"If you know anything you must tell me."

He shook his head. "Everyone knew they were in love. Didn't you?"

"I guess, but I didn't know they'd do something stupid like running away together."

"Where would they have gone?" he asked.

"I don't know. We don't even know if they're together for certain. It seems a huge coincidence that they both choose this day to leave without telling anyone where they're going."

"She's only been missing since this morning, right?"

Joy nodded. "Just since this morning. But she's never done this before."

"Did she have an argument with anybody last night?"

"Not that I can think of. Nothing unusual anyway. We're always having small squabbles between ourselves." She thought back to last night. "There were no arguments last night at all. You've spent some time with Jonathon, what do you think?"

He shook his head. "I don't know. I'm a bit shocked. What should we do?"

Joy adjusted her *kapp.* "Apart from drive around the streets looking, or … I don't know what to do."

Isaac said, "Have you had a good look right around the orchard? What if she's fallen asleep in the barn or something?"

"She's never done that before."

"Let's go back to your place and have a good look around to see if we can find her, *jah?*"

"Okay. And if she's not there we'll have to do something."

He nodded. "Agreed. Let's go."

CHAPTER 14

TWO UNSUCCESSFUL HOURS LATER, Florence felt like she was going to burst with worry. "I just don't know what to do now." She held her throbbing head and longed for the lavender oil she massaged on her temples when she felt this way.

"Maybe we should go to the police?"

"But I'm not sure they're together. If only I had proof then I might go to the police. But I don't know."

"It sounds pretty likely they're together." He looked at his navigation system. "We've got a couple more places to try. They're out of town a bit."

Florence nodded. "Let's go."

~

ISAAC AND JOY pulled up at her house. They left their buggies and walked toward each other.

Isaac looked across at the sheds. "Have you been through each and every one of the sheds?"

"I haven't and I don't know about the other girls either. We've called out and she hasn't answered."

"Let's look through them—carefully."

"Okay."

They looked through the shed where they stored the apples, the shed where they made the cider, and the shed where they stored odds and ends that didn't belong in the barn.

Lastly, they came to the barn. Isaac pushed open the double doors of the barn and called out to Honor. There was no reply. They looked in every stall, behind an old buggy that was pushed up to one side, behind all the hay bales, and she was nowhere to be seen.

"What about up there?" He pointed to the unused hayloft.

"I'm not going up there and that ladder hasn't been used in years. It's rickety."

"I'll have to go up and see if she's there."

She stood and watched him climbing the ladder placing each foot carefully on one rung after another. He finally reached far enough so he could view the loft. Then she heard a loud hiss and Isaac yelled out and leaned back nearly falling off the ladder.

"There's a large ginger cat up there." He made his way down the ladder.

Joy giggled. "That's Rochester, one of our barn cats."

"He nearly killed me. Anyway, she's not up there."

"Come down slowly." She held the ladder.

When he put his shoe on the second-to-last rung it went straight through it. Joy jumped forward and tried to steady him, but he was too heavy and they ended up on the floor of the barn together. He laughed and she jumped to her feet.

"Are you okay, Isaac? I'm so sorry. I should've caught you."

"*Nee.* I would've squashed you." He sat up and smiled at her. "I'm fine. No harm done."

"I told you that ladder wasn't safe. No one's used it in years. It's rotted through."

She put out her hands and helped him to his feet. Once he was standing, she pulled her hands away. It could've turned into a time for romance, but not when her sister was missing.

"Have you looked through the *haus?"* he asked.

"Of course we did. We looked in every cupboard, every room, and under every bed. She's just not there, not anywhere."

"What about her friends? Have you checked with them?"

"Florence went to them this morning. If she found her she would've been back by now. Shall we drive around the roads?"

"Yeah, let's do it. Will you come in my buggy?"

"Jah, okay. I'll just tell *Mamm* that's where we're going and see if she's heard any news yet."

"That sounds like a good plan. I'll wait in the buggy."

CHAPTER 15

WHEN FLORENCE and Carter arrived at the last bus stop and there was nowhere left to check, the two of them sat in his car in silence. He parked and turned off his engine, and then looked over at Florence. "Well, what should we do now?"

"I don't know what to do. We've run out of places to look."

"Perhaps she's home by now?"

She bit her lip. "I hope so. Can you take me home?"

"Sure."

"If she's there, she's going to be in the biggest trouble."

He chuckled.

She looked over at him. "What's funny?"

"Go easy on her. She's a teenager and sometimes it's hard to adjust to things."

Annoyance welled within Florence. How could he possibly understand what it was like growing up in a large family? Discipline and routine were the threads that held the fabric of family life together. “What things?”

“Life and such. Making mistakes is part of growing up.”

Florence didn't say anything because Carter didn't understand their ways, but if Honor had been out somewhere with Jonathon she would be grounded for the rest of her life!

He glanced at her. "You must be hungry by now."

She put a hand over her stomach. "I couldn't eat a thing."

"Are you sure? Because I know this nice little diner where we could get something to eat."

"I can't eat when my sister's missing."

Then Florence felt bad because he had gone to a lot of trouble driving her around and he was probably starving. "Are you hungry?"

He looked over at her and then started his engine. "I'm always hungry."

"We can stop then if you'd like to."

"It's okay. I think I'll be able to last until I get home." He moved his car onto the road.

When he pulled up at her house, he said, "Can you do me a favor?"

"What is it?" She opened the door and stayed seated.

"Stop by this afternoon and let me know if she's been found?"

"Sure. I'll do that."

"And let me know if you need me to drive you anywhere else."

"Thank you. I appreciate it. And thank you for what you've done today."

He gave her a nod and then she got out of the car. By the time she got to her front door, his car was already at the end of the driveway. When she pushed the door open and saw Mamm standing in front of her, she knew at once that Honor hadn't returned.

"You didn't find her?" *Mamm* asked.

Florence shook her head and moved further into the

house. "Our new neighbor from next door drove me to all the stations – all the bus stations and even the train station. I couldn't see either of them anywhere."

Mamm scrunched her brows and peered into her face. "*Either* of them?"

Florence gulped. She had forgotten Mamm didn't know the full story. "Jonathon is also missing."

Mamm went ashen and hurried over to sit down on the couch. "Do you think they're together?" she asked. "You do, don't you?"

Florence wished she could tell her no. "That is my fear."

"What will we do, Florence?"

"I'm not sure." She looked around. "Where is everyone?"

"Joy is driving around with Isaac trying to find her. Hope is upstairs, I think ... or in the kitchen?"

"Should we tell the bishop what's happened?"

Mamm shook her head. *"Nee,* not yet. We'll wait and see if Isaac and Joy find her."

CHAPTER 16

IT WAS mid-afternoon and Florence was peeling potatoes for dinner when she heard the phone in the barn. She threw down the paring knife and ran as fast as she could to the barn hoping the call would bring news of Honor.

"Hello," she said breathlessly as she held the receiver up to her ear.

"Florence."

"Is this you, Mercy?"

"It's me. You know Honor isn't there?"

"Jah, we've been looking everywhere. Have you heard from her?"

"That's why I'm calling. She told me not to let anybody know, but she's run away with Jonathon."

Now that she knew it for sure, Florence felt doubly worse. "That's what I thought had happened. Do you know where they are?"

"I know they're coming here. They were getting on the Greyhound and it stops at Hartford, Connecticut. I only found that out because she was talking to me and I overheard a man telling her they'd missed the bus. She was still talking to me when he told her to stay there and he'd find out when the next bus was leaving. After that, I'm not sure what their immediate plans are, but she told me they were both going to live as *Englischers* until she's old enough to get married. Then they'll come back to the community."

Florence sighed, fearing they might never find them. "Did she say what the expected arrival time of the bus was or when it was leaving?"

"*Nee.* She only called me about half an hour ago, but it took me all this time to find our home phone number. I forgot it. I had to get—"

"Okay, tell me that story later—is there anything else I need to know?"

"I can't think of anything, but I'll call back if I do."

"*Denke,* Mercy." She hung up the receiver and ran back to tell her stepmother what was going on.

Mamm stared at her after she'd told her what Mercy had said. "Can you drive there and try to find them?"

"I could, but do you think we should call the authorities? They'd have a better chance of finding them. I mean, she's only young."

"*Nee.* I don't want anybody else involved. It'll bring shame on the family."

"Okay." *Of course.* She had known her stepmother was going to say that.

"In my address book by the phone I have three numbers of drivers we've used in the past. Call them and see if any of them can take you now."

Florence knew that the chances of getting a driver at that short notice was remote, but she knew where there was a car and a driver available. "I'll see if the man next door can drive me there."

"*Jah,* okay, but hurry."

"Hope, make me a sandwich please while I get ready."

"Can I come too?"

"Nee, stay with *Mamm* and help her finish fixing dinner, please."

"Okay." Hope jumped up from her chair at the kitchen table, and then Florence ran upstairs taking them two at a time. Once in her room, she grabbed her thickest coat and her black over-bonnet to keep out the cold. When she got downstairs again Hope was coming out of the kitchen with her sandwich.

"It's only peanut butter."

"That's fine. Anything is better than nothing."

"Should I put it in something for you or will you just have it like this?"

"Like this." She grabbed it and yelled goodbye over her shoulder and then set off through the orchard hoping and praying that Carter would be home and that he'd take her where she wanted to go. It was late and she felt awful for asking him, but it was an emergency.

Florence was relieved when she saw his car outside and a light on in the house. She knocked on his door and he opened it.

He searched her face before she spoke. "Is she home yet?" he asked almost timidly as though he knew what her response was going to be."

"No, but my newly married sister called me because Honor called her and told her where she was going."

He sighed. "That was a big mistake on Honor's part if she truly didn't want to be found. Sounds like she wants to be found deep down. If she is with—"

"Jah, she is and they're heading to Hartford."

He slowly nodded.

She hoped he might've recognized the urgency of the situation and offered to drive her, but he hadn't. "I hate to ask this again, but it is an emergency. Could you drive me to the bus station at Hartford? They're going by Greyhound."

"Sure. Of course. Right now?"

"Yes, right now. It's okay if you can't. I do have the names of some drivers, but I just thought it would be quicker to ask you first since it's such short notice."

"Let's go."

He reached inside the house and pulled his coat off the hook by the door, flicked off the light, and then took keys out of his pocket and locked his front door. They then walked to his car and he clicked a remote control to unlock it.

"It's unlocked," he said.

Once again, she slid into the comfort of the black leather car seat.

When he was beside her with his belt fastened, he pressed some buttons on his navigation system. "Connecticut. It's three and a half hours away."

"Hartford, my sister said."

He pressed some more buttons. "Hmm, make that four and a half hours. There seems to be a bus and a train station combo. We'll make our way there."

She put on her seatbelt, happy he hadn't changed his mind when he saw how far away it was. "Thanks so much for doing this."

"I'm glad to be of some help. It's nice to be useful." He drove down the driveway.

NOT FAR INTO their lengthy journey, the annoying side of Carter reared its head and reminded Florence that he was very much an *Englischer.*

He drummed his fingers on the console between them while he steered the car with one hand. "One of the bonnet sisters has fallen from grace, eh?"

"Don't say that; she hasn't. She's temporarily lost her way."

He raised both hands in the air. "Potatoes potahtoes."

"Please use both hands to drive." She was so worried about Honor that she felt her head would burst.

"They say the first few hours someone goes missing is the most vital. That's why I think you should go to the police."

"Please, I don't mean to be rude, but please don't speak."

"Sorry." Then he started whistling. After ten minutes of that, he made a suggestion. "Shall we stop and get coffee?"

She stared at him. Was he serious? It was going to be a long drive, she reminded herself, and perhaps he was tired. "Do you need one?"

"Not really. I just thought it would be nice."

"I'd rather just get her out of Jonathon's clutches as soon as possible. If we miss her by one minute or even one second, I'll never forgive myself."

"I'll make a few calls to see when the bus from Lancaster is expected."

"Yes, please do that." It was a good idea to see if they should hurry or whether they could take their time. Also, it would stop his whistling.

"What time did you say they left?" he asked.

"I really don't know, except that they missed the early one. I don't even know how many buses go there a day. Maybe only one or two. That's what I'm hoping."

In less than two minutes he was getting information from the station.

CHAPTER 17

HONOR LOOKED OVER AT JONATHON, not sure of why he was angry with her. She wasn't going to put up with it.

"I can't understand why you called your sister. You already told me you couldn't trust any of them. Are you sure you can trust Mercy?"

Honor shrugged. "I don't know, but I didn't want anyone to think I'd been kidnapped."

He frowned at her. "What about the letter? I told you to write a letter."

"Calm yourself down. I did and I gave it to Joy."

"Good. How did you stop her from reading it?"

"I just told her not to."

"And, what else?"

"That's all."

Jonathon moved uncomfortably in his seat. "If someone gave me something like that I'd read it just as soon as they turned their back. I wouldn't be able to help myself."

"Joy's not like that. She always does what she says she's going to do. I told her she'd know when to give the note to *Mamm.*"

"Didn't she ask questions?"

"Nee." Honor shook her head.

"Weird."

"She is a little weird. That's the word that best describes her. She's not like the rest of us sisters."

"I don't mean she's weird, I mean the situation. I thought you'd leave the note on your pillow or something. Joy could lose it or forget about it."

Honor frowned at him. He was already in a bad mood because she'd caused them to miss the first bus, by insisting to speak with Mercy, and now he was upset about the letter. If she wanted to be scolded, she needn't have left home. "I did what I believed was best. If you're unhappy with me I'll get on the next bus home. I don't need you, you know."

"I'm sorry, I've just got a lot on my mind. This is a big thing that we're doing and it's a lot of pressure. I'm doing it all for us. If we're found we'll both be in a lot of trouble, but especially me."

"Are you sure we'll be able to hide out for a whole year?"

"I don't know. We've got to give it a try. It's the only way we can be together until you're old enough for me to marry you. I'm pretty sure we have to wait until you're eighteen, and if you're younger than that you need a parent's approval."

"We're not going to get any approval now. Maybe I should've stayed at home and *Mamm* would've let me get married as soon as I could. I would've nagged her until she gave in."

"It's too far away. A year is too long. We can't deviate now from the path we've set out on. We've already burned our bridges. You with your family and me with your family and especially with Mark. I left the job without warning and left the place I was staying."

"Left your stable you mean." She giggled.

"We've both left everything and by now everyone knows

we've gone. How long do you think it'll take them to figure out we're together?"

"Humph. They won't figure it out until they read my note."

"Let's just stick to the plan and stop looking back. I'll lease us a place to live. Firstly, I'll have to get a job. I've got a little money, but that'll be chewed up real fast."

"I can work."

"Nee. They'll want ID and a social security number."

"I'll work somewhere where they won't ask for that, or work for myself selling things at a stall. That's what I've always done."

"Maybe."

When another passenger turned around and looked at Honor, she pulled off her *kapp.*

"What are you doing?" he whispered.

"Everyone's looking at me. I want to blend in."

"I agree but wait until we stop and you can change into other clothes."

"You did bring *Englisch* clothes for me, didn't you?"

"Jah, I did." He patted his backpack that was by his feet.

She unbraided her hair and it fell down her back in waves. He ran his fingers through it. "Your hair is so beautiful."

"Is it?"

"It sure is."

CHAPTER 18

When Isaac and Joy had no success finding Honor, he took her home and then she collected Cherish and Favor from the markets.

Once they got home and unhitched the buggy, having no idea that Florence wasn't home, it was business as usual for Joy. "Give the money bag to Florence because she's got to put aside the rent for tomorrow."

"I will," said Cherish. "Give it to me, Favor."

Favor held the black money bag high in the air. "I'm older than you. I'll take it."

Cherish did her best to grab it out of Favor's hands, but she was too short. Favor giggled and then ran into the house with Cherish at her heels. Joy shook her head at them and started rubbing down the horse.

When Joy walked inside, she was met by her mother who was in tears. *Mamm* told Joy that Florence had gone to Connecticut to bring Honor home, and that Honor had run away with Jonathon.

Joy did her best to calm her *mudder*. "Leave it to Florence. She'll do it. I'm confident *Gott* has His hand on the situation."

Over *Mamm's* shoulder, she saw Favor and Cherish roll their eyes, but she didn't care. They always did that when she talked about *Gott,* but she really was sure He would help them.

"Hope's got the dinner ready." *Mamm* sniffed.

"Great. I'm starving and it smells so good."

Once they sat down to dinner, the conversation was about Honor until it turned to the week's earnings.

"Florence isn't here so what happens to the earnings? Will you look after it, Joy? You're the next oldest."

"Hmm. I'm not too good with numbers."

"It's not numbers it's money," Cherish said. "Where did you put the bag, Favor?"

"You took it." Favor glared at Cherish. "As soon as we got inside you took it. You grabbed the bag out of my hands."

Cherish bit her lip. "I gave it to Joy."

"Nee, you didn't. I would've remembered that."

Mamm said, "Stop arguing. We're all upset about Honor." She turned to Joy. "Perhaps you don't remember that Cherish gave it to you?"

"Nee, she didn't. I was the one who told them to give the money to Florence. I didn't know Florence would be off somewhere."

"I remember Favor giving it to me but I can't remember where I put it."

"Nee! You snatched it from me," Favor said. "I didn't *give* it to you."

Joy sighed. "It's got to be in the *haus* somewhere. It'll turn up. As long as we find it by tomorrow morning it'll be okay, because Mr. Pettigrew will have to be paid."

Mamm said, "Just have a little break, Cherish, sit down and think where you put it."

"I am sitting down."

"I meant for you to relax and have a sit-down after

dinner. Don't think about it for a minute and then try to remember where you were when Favor gave it to you and what happened next."

Favor shook her head and muttered, "What's the use? I might as well not speak at all because no one listens to anything I say."

Cherish nodded. "I'll do that after dinner, *Mamm.*"

Over the after-dinner washing up, Joy heard someone crying in the living room. She walked out to see Cherish crying and their mother comforting her.

"What's wrong?" Joy at first assumed Cherish was trying to take the attention away from Honor since Cherish thought everything should revolve around her.

"She can't find the money," *Mamm* told her while Cherish sobbed into her hands.

Joy sat on the other side of her. "You're getting yourself worked up. You're not going to remember when you're upset."

"My mind's just blank. I can't remember anything after when she gave me the bag. What if someone came into the *haus* and stole it?"

"No one would've done that. Someone would've seen them."

"That's the only answer I can think of because it's gone."

Now Joy was worried. With Florence and Honor absent, it was her job as the eldest in the house to look after the finances and if neither of them were back by tomorrow, she'd have to deliver the rent money. The only other way to get money was to draw money from the family's account, but for that to happen Florence needed to sign for it and she was halfway to Connecticut by now.

Joy said to Cherish. "I'll help you look all through the *haus.* Let's look through your bedroom first."

"I've looked there and Favor and Hope have even helped me."

"Have you looked through the clothes you were wearing today?"

"I was in these clothes and the bag isn't here." Cherish stood up and shook her dress and apron out. "Anyway, it was too big to be hiding somewhere, that's why I think someone has come in and stolen it."

Mamm shook her head. "No one's been near the place."

"They have." Cherish looked at Joy. "You came home with Isaac. You told us he helped you look for Honor here."

"Don't be ridiculous. Isaac didn't even come inside. Neither was the money here then because you weren't home from the markets."

"I don't think he took it. I don't, but I mean someone must've because it's not here. It couldn't have just vanished, could it?" Cherish sobbed again. "Everything's gone wrong for me. I can't believe Honor and Jonathon are together. They can't be. He liked me, not her. I was so sure of it."

Mamm frowned at Cherish and then looked at Joy who didn't know what to say.

Joy finally said, "Go to sleep, and we'll worry about the missing money in the morning."

Through tear-filled eyes, Cherish looked at her. "But don't you have to take the rent in tomorrow morning?"

"I do, but I'm confident it will turn up by then. We'll all pray, *jah?"*

"We will, Joy," *Mamm* said. "We will."

"Don't worry, Cherish, just go to bed."

"I don't think I'll be able to sleep. I'll be so worried and not only about the money."

Joy wasn't even going to ask what the other thing was

that her sister was worried about. "Put it all out of your mind, say your prayers, and have a good night's sleep. You'll need all your energy for tomorrow when Florence brings Honor home."

After *Mamm* and the other girls went to bed, Joy sat alone by the fire. She had no idea where the money was and what Cherish had absent-mindedly done with it. Joy bit her lip and stared into the flickering flames in the fireplace. Would Florence be able to find Honor and bring her home?

Joy closed her eyes and thought about the positives of the situation. At least they knew that Honor was still alive and well because she'd called Mercy. And, Honor was with Jonathon and that was probably better than running away by herself—safer for her, at least.

CHAPTER 19

"Wake up. We're here."

Florence opened her eyes and with a jolt, realized where she was—in Carter Braithwaite's car. Then the horror of Honor having disappeared flooded back to her. "We're here already?"

"You've been asleep for hours. I stopped for gas and you still didn't wake."

"I must've really dozed off. I'm sorry." She blinked and when she saw he was staring at her, she said, "It's hardly fair on you for me to fall asleep."

"It's okay. I was entertained by listening to you snore." He chuckled and got out of the car.

She grimaced, then unbuckled her seat belt and opened the door. Her neck ached from falling asleep at a funny angle. Rubbing her neck, she looked over the top of the car at him. "Are we on time?"

He glanced at his watch. "We're early."

Florence looked around. "Where to?"

He looked around and pointed to a sign. "Arrivals."

Once they were in the station itself, they had to walk through the food outlets to get to the arrivals.

"I'm starving. I've got to eat something." He headed to buy food and she hurried after him.

"But what if we miss them?"

He looked at his watch. "The bus isn't due for another fifteen minutes. Do you want anything?"

"No thank you." Her stomach churned too much to think about food. He ordered a large black coffee and a hot dog with mustard.

"The vegetarian thing didn't last long."

His mouth turned down at the corners. "I don't think there's real meat in these things."

Florence grimaced at that thought, and he laughed.

While they stood there waiting for the food, Florence said, "I hope they're on the bus and I hope they didn't change their minds and get off somewhere else." She held her stomach. "Or what if they just told Mercy they were coming here and it wasn't true?"

He drew his eyebrows together. "You mean we could've driven all this way for nothing?"

"It's possible." She'd feel bad for having him drive that long distance if Honor and Jonathon weren't on that bus, but all she could do was follow the lead she'd been given.

The server handed him his hot dog and at the same time his black coffee was ready down at the end of the counter.

He took hold of his food and then grabbed his coffee. "Let's go and wait somewhere for the bus." A few steps along, he said, "There's the bus from Lancaster. The one that's just pulled up. It's a few minutes early."

He took a large bite of his hot dog as they hurried over. Then Florence saw Honor step out of the bus in front of Jonathon.

Florence gasped.

"Is that her without her bonnet? The one with the really long hair?" Carter asked before he took his last bite.

"Yes, that's her." Florence sent up a prayer of thanks. It was devastating to see her sister with no head covering, but she was so pleased they'd found her. "Let's go." Florence felt like her legs were so heavy she couldn't move, and then she felt her chest constrict and couldn't breathe for a moment.

Carter threw his coffee away along with the hotdog wrapper. Then he held onto her arm. "Are you okay? You're as white as a sheet. You should eat something."

"I'm fine." Florence forced herself to take a slow deep breath, blew it out, summoned all her strength and stepped out.

Together they walked over and when Honor looked up and saw her, she froze to the spot and her jaw dropped open. When Florence stood in front of her, Honor gulped. "What are *you* doing here?"

"Bringing you home."

"I don't want to go anywhere. I'm going to stay with Jonathon." Jonathon stood beside her.

"That's right. We're together now."

Florence ignored Jonathon completely.

"No, you're not, you're coming home with me." Florence then stared at Jonathon and he looked away, looking dreadfully guilty. "What were you thinking, Jonathon? She's a child. She's only seventeen. I could have you arrested for kidnapping."

"Wait a minute. I didn't kidnap her. She wanted to come. We're going to get married."

Carter stepped forward and said to Jonathon. "Wake up to yourself, man. Do you know how much trouble you're in?" He shook his finger at him. "She's a minor. That makes—"

Florence put her hand lightly on Carter's shoulder. "Let's just get her out of here."

Jonathon said, "She's not a child. She's seventeen. Legally old enough to get married in some states."

Carter then shook his fist in front of Jonathon's face. "If I find you've laid one finger on her I'll come back and find you."

Jonathon hung his head. "I haven't touched her. It's not like that."

"You better be telling the truth." Carter turned to Florence and gave her a nod. "Let's go."

"I'm not going. I'm staying with Jonathon," Honor whined. She stamped her boot onto the asphalt.

Jonathon sighed. "They're right, Honor. We'll have to wait until you're older. Then we'll be together. There's no point if they're going to be so against us. Your mother would never give her approval."

"Nee. Let's just do what we were going to do. We can't let them stop us."

Carter said to Jonathon, "You'll be in big trouble if she doesn't come with us now."

"You'll have to go with them, Honor. We'll wait until your birthday."

"That's too far away," she whimpered, tears welling in her eyes.

Florence grabbed hold of Honor's arm and started walking.

Jonathon took a step forward and Carter gave a head-shake and moved to block his way. Then Jonathon called out to Honor, "I'll be waiting for you, Honor."

"I'll see you soon," she called through her tears, looking back over her shoulder while being dragged away.

When they got to the car, Carter opened the back and the front passenger doors. Once Honor was in the back and had angrily fastened her seatbelt, Florence got into the front seat. Carter pushed a button on his door panel before starting the engine and driving away from the station. Florence realized the button was a child-safety feature that prevented Honor from opening her door.

Honor whimpered, "How did you find me?"

"I got a call telling me where you might be headed."

"It was Mercy, wasn't it? She's the only one who could've told you where I was going. I've gone all that way for nothing because of Mercy."

"You're the one in the wrong. Don't go making out someone else is to blame for this."

"I'm not, it's just that I know it was Mercy and I'll never trust her again."

"*Mamm* and I will never trust you again. Not after this. What were you thinking? You're a child." When Honor didn't answer, Florence turned around and saw her quietly sobbing into her hands. Florence looked over at Carter and he looked at her with an 'I don't know what to do either' look on his face.

Florence figured it was time to be silent. They'd gotten her back and now Honor needed to go home and stop thinking about Jonathon. The sooner the better.

A few miles along, Honor asked, "Why did you let the driver talk to Jonathon like that?"

"He deserved it and more. Anyway, he's not 'the driver,' he's our new neighbor. He's Carter Braithwaite. Carter, this is Honor."

"Pleased to meet you, Honor." Carter's voice was cheerful and Honor merely responded with a groan. Then Carter said, "I don't know about you two, but I'm starving."

"Me too. I think I can eat now," Florence felt better for Honor's sake and for Wilma's. Wilma would be thrilled to have her daughter home.

"I just want to go home," Honor said.

"That's too bad," Carter said. "We're going to stop for some food. Florence hasn't eaten for hours."

"Yes, that looks like as good a place as any. I'm sure you don't care what you eat, Florence, as long as it's something."

"That's right."

As Carter ordered the food at the window, Honor leaned forward over the seat and said to Florence, "Thanks for ruining my life."

Florence turned around and glared at her. "In a few months, you'll be thanking me for saving it. Be sure to put your prayer *kapp* back on before we get home."

Honor flopped back into her seat and the rest of the drive home was silent.

CHAPTER 20

CARTER DROVE UP THE BAKERS' driveway and stopped at the front door. Honor pulled on her door handle but nothing happened. She looked at it curiously. Carter subtly pushed the release button in his door panel and when she pulled the handle again, the door opened. She jumped out and hurried to the house.

Florence was pleased to see that Honor had braided her hair, pinned it up, and put her prayer *kapp* on at some point in the journey. She turned to Carter. "I can never thank you enough for doing this."

He blinked his bloodshot eyes. "Anytime—not too soon, though. I'll need a good sleep first if she runs away again."

"Sleep. What a thought. That's the first thing I'll be doing." She unbuckled her seat belt and climbed out of the car. "Thanks, Carter."

"You're welcome."

She walked to the door to hear *Mamm* say to Honor, "Why did you run off like that?"

"It's what I chose to do. That's all. I don't want to keep hearing about it. I'm back now. You got what you wanted."

"You sound like you don't even care how worried we've been."

"What's it got to do with you? It's my life. Florence keeps telling me I'm too young. I'm old enough to know what I want. Jonathon said I'm legally old enough to marry if we lived in a different state."

"Go up to your room now until you learn some manners." Florence overheard *Mamm* and knew she was doing her best to be firm. Honor charged up to her bedroom and then her mother walked to the bottom of the stairs and called out, "You're not old enough to know anything." She turned to Florence. "*Denke* for bringing her back."

"Of course." Florence collapsed into the couch. She felt like she hadn't slept for days.

"Where did you find her?"

"Getting off a bus in Connecticut, with Jonathon."

Wilma gasped. "So, it's true?" When Florence nodded, Wilma all but collapsed into the nearest chair.

"They say they're in love and want to be together." Florence didn't even like saying the words. What Honor was feeling wasn't love, not a mature ready-for-marriage love, and Jonathon … Jonathon was so unprincipled that he needed some kind of discipline from someone. Perhaps his bishop needed to know what had gone on, or their own bishop, but she knew her stepmother wouldn't accept that because that would mean dragging Honor into it too. Wilma would prefer if it were all swept under the rug. Floating over the top of issues was how the woman coped with life.

Mamm said, "I can't believe that Jonathon didn't put a stop to the foolish girl's ideas."

"I'd say it was he who put the idea into her head in the first place. I wouldn't blame Honor too much. Jonathon's the older one and should've had more sense."

"Where is he now?"

"I don't know—and quite frankly I don't care."

"He won't come back here, will he?"

"He wouldn't be brave enough to show his face around here again after what he's done."

"That's mean, Florence." Honor's voice rang out from the top of the stairs.

"Go back to your room," *Mamm* said. "I can't believe you just ran off like that and left us worried. We had no idea what happened to you."

"I wrote you the letter so you wouldn't worry."

"What letter?"

Honor walked down two stairs and sat down on the top step. "I wrote a note and gave it to Joy to give to you."

Mamm and Florence looked at one another.

"That's the first time we're hearing about this," Florence said.

"We'll talk to Joy about that in the morning."

"It's morning now."

"Later this morning, after we've all had some sleep."

Then Joy came out of her bedroom. "You're home! Where were you?"

Honor didn't say anything.

"Joy," *Mamm* called out.

Joy walked down the stairs. "*Nee*. I haven't found it ... um, yet?"

"What?" asked *Mamm.*

"The money. Isn't that what you were talking about?" Joy asked.

"Do you know anything about a note or a letter?"

"You mean the one Honor gave me?"

Honor ran down the stairs. "See? It's true!"

"Be quiet," *Mamm* told her. "Don't wake the rest of your sisters. Joy, why didn't you tell us about this note?"

"I couldn't. She said it was a secret."

Honor said to Joy, "I couldn't tell you I was running away, so I said, 'Here's a letter. You'll know when to give it to Mamm.'"

"I'm sorry. I didn't know I was supposed to give it to *Mamm* when you were missing. You should've been clearer."

All Florence could do was shake her head at all of them. At *Mamm* for telling Honor to go to her room and now saying nothing about her being in the living room, and at Joy for not realizing what an emergency was and for not giving *Mamm* the letter, and at Honor for doing what she'd done in the first place.

Feeling like she didn't fit into the family, Florence got a new burst of energy and jumped to her feet. She wanted to yell at the top of her lungs and tell everyone to wake up to themselves, but she held it together. Now she understood why Earl had just up and left after *Dat's* death. "I need some fresh air."

Mamm looked up at her in surprise, while the two girls stared at her, looking for all the world like a pair of owls. "But ... but ... It's dark outside," *Mamm* said.

"I'm not going far. I just need to get outside." Everything was so much harder for Florence because *Mamm* wasn't strict enough. Instead of being one of the girls, she'd had to step up and practically become the mother. That had resulted in her not having a sisterly relationship with any of her half-sisters.

If she'd had a different relationship with Honor, they could've talked and Honor might have told her what she had been thinking and feeling. Florence would've had a chance to help her see sense. It had been so 'over-the-top' wrong for her, a young unmarried girl, to run off with Jonathon.

Florence stepped off the porch and pulled her shawl higher around her shoulders. As she looked up at the stars in the dark sky, a gust of frosty wind bit into her cheeks. She knew she should be grateful to be part of the family, but she couldn't help feeling that if her father were still alive everything would be so much better. Honor wouldn't have dared run away.

Everything had changed when *Dat* died. Her world had turned upside down. She had lost not only him, but she'd lost her two older brothers as well. Earl had abruptly left for Ohio, and then Mark announced he was getting married. Mark had been on *rumspringa* when *Dat* died and Florence was sure that him marrying Christina right after was a reaction. There was surely no other reason Mark would have married Christina. She wasn't very pleasant.

Florence's biggest fear was that Honor would run away again. She'd shown no signs of repentance.

"Are you okay, Florence?" *Mamm* came outside with a flashlight.

"It's just too much, *Mamm* and I'm worried she'll try it again. We haven't been hard enough on her."

"I'll call Mercy and tell her we've found her."

"Denke, Mamm. I didn't even think of that. And can you call Mark and Christina as well? It's late, but they might be lying awake, worried."

"Sure. I'll call them."

While *Mamm* made the calls, Florence paced up and down, too worked up to relax. When *Mamm* came back out of the barn after making the calls, she said, "I told Mark and he was relieved."

"And what about Mercy?"

"Mercy said Jonathon arrived at his parents' *haus.* He's staying there for a few days and then he's going to go up north to get away for a while."

Florence let out a sigh of relief, but she knew that Honor would hate to hear Jonathon had made plans that didn't include her.

CHAPTER 21

Florence only had about two hours sleep and woke up at first light. She pulled on her apron, went downstairs and noticed the fire was still going. Her mother or one of the girls must've been up in the small hours and put on more logs. Once she'd rearranged the fire and added another log, she headed into the kitchen to make coffee. She was surprised to see Wilma sitting at the table sipping tea. "You couldn't get any sleep either?"

Her stepmother shook her head. "No sleep at all."

"Why don't you go back to bed now?"

"I feel sick with everything that's happened."

"I'm making *kaffe.* Do you want some, or would you rather have more tea?"

"I can't take any more hot tea. I'll try some *kaffe.*"

When the coffee was made, Florence sat down with her stepmother.

"What you don't know is that there's another problem."

Florence sighed and couldn't believe her ears. "What's that?"

"The week's takings from the market is missing."

Florence stared at her stepmother, eyebrows raised almost to her hairline. "What on earth? How did that happen?"

"The girls had it when they got home—Cherish and Favor went to the markets yesterday and Joy drove them there and back. They had it when they got home. The money was in the usual black bag. It's somewhere here in the *haus,* but no one can find it anywhere."

Florence was relieved to hear that it was in the house, at least. "Well, if it's here we'll be able to find it. Has the rent been paid?"

"Nee, that has to be done today."

"I'll do that today after the girls have gone to the markets. I'll follow them in."

"Okay."

Cherish walked into the kitchen. "I see Honor's back."

"That's right. We found her where Mercy said she'd be and now—"

"What about Jonathon?"

"Mercy said he's staying with his family for a few days and then going up north for a bit."

Cherish tilted her chin upward. "Up north where?"

"I don't know. I didn't care enough to ask," Florence said.

Cherish frowned. "Are you sure he's staying with his family for a few days?"

"That's right."

Cherish walked over and poured herself some coffee out of the plunger pot and sat down with them.

Florence said, "About this missing money."

Cherish groaned. "Yeah, did *Mamm* tell you all about it?"

"Jah. You had it when you got home and then it disappeared?"

"That's right and I've looked everywhere."

"I'll help you look after breakfast."

"I really don't have anywhere else to look."

"It's obviously somewhere you haven't looked."

Cherish wrinkled her nose. "Obviously."

"Who's working on the stall today?"

"Not me. I refuse to go today. Hope didn't go yesterday so it'll have to be Hope and someone else."

Florence looked at *Mamm,* who said, "Hope and Joy can go today."

WHEN THEY'D FINISHED BREAKFAST, Honor was still asleep. Florence organized the girls to look through every inch of the house for the missing money. Her domain was the living room. She decided to start with the couch, picked up a cushion, and found the black bag. She looked inside to see all the rolled-up notes and called out, "I found it, as soon as I started looking. No one looked very hard."

Everyone hurried into the living room.

"Where was it?" Cherish asked.

"Under the cushion on the couch."

Cherish shook her head. "I don't even remember putting it there. I must've put it there as a hiding place."

"At least it's found now," Favor said.

FLORENCE WAITED for Joy and Hope to head out to the market stall, and then she traveled in a separate buggy to pay the rent to Mr Pettigrew. It was a little surprising that Cherish hadn't asked to come for the ride, but Florence figured she wanted to ask Honor about Jonathon as soon as she woke. Jonathon seemed to be Cherish's favorite subject at the moment. For the life of her, Florence couldn't figure out why her two sisters thought Jonathon was so great.

CHAPTER 22

ONCE THE RENT had been paid, Florence was tempted to stop and have a quiet coffee and a piece of cake by herself in a café before going home. What stopped her was the fear that an argument would break out between Honor and Cherish over Jonathon. She had to go home to be the peacemaker.

When she was about halfway home, she saw an *Englisch* girl a ways up ahead, hitchhiking with a bag slung over her shoulder and a small dog by her feet. The dog looked suspiciously like Caramel. And the girl ...

The girl disappeared behind a tree. Florence drove until she was even with the tree, pulled the buggy over to the side and got out to take a look. She discovered Cherish hiding behind a clump of trees. Florence couldn't believe her eyes and kept staring at her in horror. Her long hair was braided and wound onto the base of her head and pinned in a messy clump, and she wore tight jeans and a loose white shirt. "What are you doing?"

"I'm leaving."

"No, you're not! Get in the buggy now."

"I won't. You can't tell me what to do anymore. I'm going and never coming back."

"Get into the buggy now!"

"No!"

Caramel jumped up on Florence, pleased to see her. Florence swooped down and lifted him into her arms and ran back to the buggy with him, knowing Cherish would never leave without Caramel.

"What are you doing? He's my dog and he's coming with me."

"If you don't get in right now I'm going back home to get *Mamm* and I'll bring her back."

"Florence, don't do this. I'm leaving and you can't stop me. If you take me home, I'm only going to leave again, and again and again. I don't want to be here anymore. I don't want to be Amish anymore. Just leave me be."

Florence drove off and her heart ached as though it was breaking. In the rear-view mirror, she saw Cherish's sad face, but what could she do? Her sister wasn't old enough to make the decision to leave.

Once Florence was home, she ran inside the house with Caramel tucked under one arm to tell her stepmother what was going on. It was another shock for her.

Then while *Mamm* got into the buggy, Florence figured they'd need backup so she called Mark from the phone in the barn. With Caramel safely inside the house, *Mamm* and she made their way back to Cherish.

"I hope she's still there," *Mamm* said.

"I did my best. She refused to get into the buggy."

"You should've dragged her."

Florence sighed and prayed that Cherish would be there. She couldn't go through with another search for a missing sister. She was already exhausted from the last one.

Fighting back tears, *Mamm* said, "I don't know where I've

gone wrong with you girls. First Honor, and now Cherish. I don't know what I'm going to do."

Florence glanced over at her. "You've done nothing wrong. You've been a perfectly *gut mudder."* When Florence looked back at the road, she was delighted to see Cherish still there, sitting right where she'd left her. "There she is. Can you see her?"

"Look at what she's wearing!" her stepmother said in disgust.

"Er ... *jah,* I forgot to mention that." Florence stopped the buggy close by and *Mamm* got out and hurried over to Cherish. Florence got out too and stayed by Wilbur, patting his neck and praying. She prayed her mother would be able to talk sense into Cherish and that her sister would get into the buggy without too many problems. After all, they couldn't physically force her into the buggy. Cherish had to see sense.

Florence heard her stepmother say, "What's gotten into you?"

"I'm leaving. And that's that."

"You can leave when you're old enough. If you want to leave us later, when you're eighteen, then that's your right to do so, but until then you have to come home with me."

Cherish then stared into the distance. "You called Mark?"

Mamm looked up to see Mark's buggy. "I didn't call him."

"I did," Florence called out.

"You should mind your own business, Florence."

"You are my business," Florence called back. "You're my *schweschder."*

Mark jumped out of his buggy and rushed toward Cherish. After a few minutes of him talking with Cherish, she agreed to go home. Florence said a silent prayer of thanks.

When they were home after an unpleasant silent trip, Cherish was sent up to her room. After Florence unhitched the buggy, she noticed Cherish's knapsack and took it into the house. When *Mamm* saw it in Florence's hands, she decided to look through it. She sat down on the couch and pulled everything out.

"Florence, look! It's make up." Her stepmother put a hand to her forehead and wept. Through tear-filled eyes, *Mamm* said, "I can't cope anymore. I think this is a job for Dagmar. She's always asking if one of you girls can come to stay with her."

Florence was shocked. Aunt Dagmar wasn't liked by any of her half-sisters. *"Dat's* older *schweschder,* you mean? Dagmar from Millersburg?"

"Jah."

"But she lives so far away and the girls aren't fond of her." When Wilma just stared at her, it clicked into place. "I see what you mean. You'd really send Cherish there? Or are you thinking about Honor?"

"Cherish needs to go. I think it's just what she needs. Can you call Dagmar and ask her if she can take her in?"

Florence was taken aback that her mother was sending Cherish away and not Honor, but at least she was disciplining someone for a change. "Sure. When do you want her to go?"

"I'll drive up there with her tomorrow if Dagmar agrees, or as soon as we can find a driver to take us."

"I'll make a few calls after I get some sleep. I'll arrange transport."

"And you'll call Dagmar?"

"Jah, sure."

"Gut. Could you do it now?"

Florence had hoped *Mamm* would change her mind. A little time would've given her a chance to think things through and maybe focus on a punishment for Honor. As far as she knew, Honor had no ramifications for running away. "Okay. I'll do it now."

"And if you can watch things here, I'll stay a couple of days with Dagmar to get Cherish settled in and then I'll come back. I'll tell Dagmar what's happened and I'll forbid Cherish to talk to Jonathon Wilkes ever again."

"It might be best not to tell Cherish what's happening until the car arrives—just in case she tries to run away again before we have everything organized."

Mamm nodded.

Florence headed to the barn and called Aunt Dagmar. She was delighted to have Cherish come to stay with her and even said yes to Cherish bringing Caramel. Dagmar also assured Florence she'd watch Cherish like a hawk and wouldn't let her talk to any man, let alone Jonathon Wilkes. As soon as Florence hung up the receiver from Dagmar, she arranged a car to take them tomorrow, and then made another quick call back to Aunt Dagmar to let her know what time they might arrive. Finally, Florence headed back into the house, drained of all energy.

When she saw Wilma asleep on the couch, she tiptoed up to her room to have a rest. Across the hallway, she heard Cherish sobbing, but had no sympathy. Every trace of emotion had been drawn out of her.

CHAPTER 23

THE NEXT MORNING, a car was due to arrive at any minute to drive them to Aunt Dagmar's farm in Millersburg.

Mamm walked down the stairs carrying a black fabric bag and set it by the front door.

"Going somewhere, *Mamm?"* Cherish asked.

"Jah and so are you. We're taking a little road trip."

Cherish rubbed her neck. "Where to?"

"To visit Aunt Dagmar."

"Nee! I'm not going there!"

"You're going to be staying there until you get over this silliness about being in love with Jonathon."

"What?" she screeched. "You're sending me away?"

"Jah, if that's what you want to call it."

Cherish shook her head. "I'm not going and there's no way you can force me."

Mamm nodded. "You are."

"I'm never going to change the way I feel about Jonathon."

Honor said, "Jonathon loves me not you. He's never been interested in you because you're a child."

Cherish's voice got louder. "Well, that's what *Mamm* and

everyone say about you. If he really loved you he wouldn't have let you come back. Or, he would've come back too."

Florence heard the conversation from the kitchen and figured she needed to help Wilma. She walked out into the living room. "This is what's happening, Cherish. You're going upstairs and throwing clothes into a bag, and you're going to stay with Aunt Dagmar until *Mamm* says you can come home."

Favor and Honor sat at the table with their mouths open, listening to everything play out.

Cherish's lips turned down at the corners. "Can I take Caramel?"

"I did ask Dagmar about Caramel and she said he could come too, but if you don't get yourself ready right now, I won't allow you to take him."

Cherish pulled a face at Florence. "Okay. I'll go. I'll get out of going to the markets and doing so many chores. It won't be so bad. Probably better than here. It won't be so bad." She went upstairs and soon came back down carrying a bag over her shoulder and holding Caramel under one arm. "I'm ready."

At that moment, the car pulled up right on time. Cherish walked out of the house without looking back at Florence and without even saying goodbye. *Mamm* hadn't told Joy and Hope what was going on before they'd left for the markets. Then she quickly told Favor and Honor what was happening.

Honor stayed put, but Favor ran past *Mamm* to say goodbye to Cherish who was now in the car waiting. Florence moved out onto the porch and *Mamm* walked out the front door and heaved a sigh.

"Denke, Florence. I don't know what I'd do without you. These girls will be the death of me one day."

Florence hugged *Mamm.* "Have a nice couple of days with Aunt Dagmar and give her my love."

"I will."

"Will you be back before Christmas? It's only days away."

"I want to be back before then, if I can."

Florence walked Wilma to the car. "Bye, Cherish."

Cherish ignored her and looked straight ahead. It seemed Cherish thought sending her off to Aunt Dagmar was all her idea.

It was a relief when they drove away. It was going to be tough for Aunt Dagmar, but she'd said she was up for the task.

"Florence, *Mamm* said I could visit my friends today." Honor asked. "That's okay, isn't it?"

"Nee." Florence folded her arms across her chest. "You should be the one going to Dagmar's."

Honor's bottom lip quivered. *"Mamm* said I could go. I'm not grounded. Did she say I was?"

Florence sighed. In *Mamm's* haste to keep Cherish out of trouble, Honor's deed had gone unpunished. "Are you certain *Mamm* said you can?"

"Jah. I apologized for what I did. *Mamm* forgave me. She knows how sorry I am and I'd never do anything like that again. That's why Cherish is being punished and not me. Cherish might try to run away again. Who knows where she'd end up? At least I had a plan."

Florence had little strength to argue, or to enforce a grounding. Convinced Honor wouldn't do it again, she decided to take the easy way out for once. "As long as you're truly repentant and not about to do it again. *Mamm* wouldn't be able to cope with it and she might inquire if Aunt Dagmar has another bedroom for you."

"I won't. Believe me."

"Okay. Go visit your friends, but you will be getting extra chores starting tonight—for several weeks."

Honor nodded.

Favor came up beside them, and said to Honor, "It's weird that Cherish likes Jonathon and you do too."

Honor agreed. "I'm so upset with her. He's in love with me."

Florence was in no mood to listen to the girls. "Seems like you'll be on your own for a while Favor. You're old enough and I'll only be gone for a few hours."

"I'm plenty old enough. Older and wiser than Cherish."

"Being wiser than Cherish wouldn't be hard at all." Florence regretted her words, but it was too late to take them back. Her two half-sisters giggled.

"Will you be out the whole day?" Favor asked Honor.

"I'll be back in time to help with the evening meal and I won't leave for a couple of hours."

"Denke. That would be good," Favor said.

"I should thank our neighbor," said Florence. "It was so good of him to drive me there and back. We were nearly a whole day and most of the night driving." She stared at Honor. "You really should get a more of a punishment for what you did."

"Nee, Florence. I've learned my lesson and I'll do those extra chores."

Florence pressed her lips together. "I'll think up some good ones for you."

The two girls walked back into the house and Florence headed to Carter's house through the orchard.

TODAY'S WALK WAS DIFFERENT. It wasn't the nice restful walk she took most afternoons. Her head was spinning from lack of sleep and her stomach still churned from the stress that Cherish had put her through.

When Carter's house came into view, she saw him getting

into his car. He looked up, saw her and straightened up. He closed his door and walked toward her. "Hello."

"Hello. I thought you would've had enough of driving for a few days."

He chuckled. "That's true, but I had a good few hours' sleep and I'm ready to face the world again."

She walked a few more steps until she stood in front of him. "I've just come to say thank you."

"You already thanked me."

"Last night was a blur. Anyway, you did such a lot for someone you don't even know."

"I know you, and now I know Honor a bit more."

"My stepmother's sent my youngest half-sister to stay with an aunt. She was becoming a handful."

"Oh really? As punishment?"

"Kind of, and to keep her away from trouble of all kinds. She had a weird childish crush on Jonathon and she's only thirteen."

"Jonathon must have something going for him. I couldn't tell just by looking at him."

"Yeah, well I don't know what that something would be."

"It must be hard to be having problems with two of your sisters."

She nodded.

He stared at her more closely. "Would you care to see my renovations now?"

She took a step back. "I really should get back home. There's so much to do."

"Some other time?"

"Yes. Bye."

He smiled at her and gave her a nod before she turned and walked away.

CHAPTER 24

FLORENCE WAS COUNTING the days until *Mamm* was back. Ada had come to the house crying when she learned that Jonathon and Honor had run away. She blamed herself because Jonathon was her nephew.

Florence then learned from Ada that Jonathon had a reputation of being unscrupulous and a dreadful flirt. It would've been nice to know that before he'd worked in their orchard around her half-sisters, but still, she couldn't turn back the clock.

In the days that *Mamm* was gone, the girls had been unusually quiet.

Honor was understandably behaving well and keeping out of Florence's way.

Florence's afternoon walks around her orchard had been brief due to the chilly weather and also due to her decision to stay away from Carter Braithwaite. Staying away from his house though, wasn't keeping him out of her head.

~

ON CHRISTMAS EVE MORNING, *Mamm* was back.

When the car pulled up, Florence's half-sisters ran out to greet their mother. Florence stayed back on the porch watching and waiting. She heaved a sigh of relief when it was clear Wilma was alone. She'd half expected Cherish would've talked her way out of staying with Aunt Dagmar. There was no doubt Cherish would've tried, but Wilma must've stayed strong and Florence was pleased. She stepped off the porch and joined in with the girls in greeting Wilma.

Florence took the bag from the driver and followed the giggling girls as they walked their mother into the house. After Florence took Wilma's bag upstairs and set it on her bed, she walked downstairs to see the girls gathered around Wilma in the living room. Two were sitting with *Mamm* on the couch, one to either side, and the others sat on the rug at her feet.

"Tea, *Mamm?"*

Wilma looked over at Florence and smiled. "Please, Florence."

"I'll boil the kettle."

"Then hurry back here so I can tell you what's been happening."

After Florence filled the kettle and lit the stove, she walked back into the living room. Hope had moved to the floor to allow her to sit on the couch next to *Mamm. "Denke,* Hope," she said as she sat down. "How's Cherish?"

"She's not happy, but then again I didn't expect she would be."

Florence was a little surprised to see a hint of a smile around *Mamm's* lips.

"Tell us everything," Favor said.

"As you know, Aunt Dagmar is very domineering and she always talks about when your *vadder* and she were young and how things were back then. They weren't allowed to get away with this and they weren't allowed to get away with that. And how their *Dat* used to beat them with a strap if they did the slightest thing wrong."

Florence nodded. "That's how things were back then for a lot of people."

Mamm said, "I've had quite an ordeal."

"Tell us."

"Cherish begged me to let her come back. I said she couldn't. Not until she got over this Jonathon nonsense."

"Jah, she should get over it," Honor said. "He'll be her *bruder*-in-law and that's all."

"Dagmar is not allowing her near a phone, and on the farm she'll only talk to people who visit, and the people at their bi-monthly meetings."

"Ach, she's going to hate that," Favor said.

"Serves her right. Jonathon loves me," Honor commented.

"Can't you let her come home?" Favor asked.

"Nee. Dagmar sews quilts and makes baskets and she's going to teach Cherish."

Florence nodded. "She'd like that. She's always asking me if she can sew."

"Now she can do that and make baskets all day except when she's doing chores on the farm," *Mamm* said.

Favor sighed. "I suppose she has Caramel with her, but when will we see her again?"

"Not for a while, I fear."

Joy sighed. "Now there's only the four of us. Oh, not counting you, Florence." Before Florence could comment, Joy kept right on talking, "I invited Isaac for dinner tonight. Is that all right?"

"Jah, that's okay. I might have a lie down to recover and then I'll find some more energy."

The kettle whistled. "I'll make you that tea first." Florence headed to the kitchen still listening to the girls talking.

"Do you want something to eat too?" Hope asked.

"Nee. I'm not hungry at the moment."

"Save it up for the nice dinner I'm cooking tonight," Honor said.

As Florence poured the boiling water onto the leaves in the teapot, she had a funny feeling about Joy and Isaac. They had been spending a lot of time together. What if they wanted to get married? *Mamm* was tired and ground down after the whole business with Cherish and Honor right on top of Mercy's wedding. Reminding herself not to cross her bridges before she got to them, she reached up into the cupboard for a cup and a saucer.

Florence put the tea items on a tray and carried them out to *Mamm.* She asked one of the girls to place the small table in front of her stepmother.

"Denke, Florence. I just realized … who's at the markets today?"

"Ada and Christina are at the stall for us. They said they'd do it because they knew you were coming home today."

Mamm smiled. "Bless their hearts. And they took their time to do that on Christmas Eve."

"They probably didn't have anything better to do," Favor said.

The other girls laughed.

"I'm sure that's not true," *Mamm* said.

Florence sat down next to her stepmother again. "I'm sure they'd have lots to do. They did it as a kindness to us."

"I'll pour the tea." Hope poured the tea for *Mamm* and then handed it to her.

Mamm had barely finished taking a sip when Joy told her that Isaac was now working in Mark's store and living in the room off from the stable where Jonathon used to live.

"Well," *Mamm* said, "things have worked out well for Isaac."

"Jah, and we heard that Jonathon has left the community," Joy said, shaking her head.

"He's heartbroken that's why," Honor said. "That's what I think, but he'll come back as soon as we can be together. He'll be back for me."

Mamm frowned. "Let's not talk about him."

CHAPTER 25

A FEW HOURS LATER, Florence found Honor in her bedroom, crying. She sat down beside her. "What's upset you?"

"*You* know. I'll never love anyone else and now he's left the community. What is wrong with everyone? I know people in the community who've married at seventeen."

"*Jah,* but they didn't run away to do it. They got permission and ... and they chose a suitable person."

Honor pouted at Florence. "I knew you wouldn't allow it and *Mamm* would do what you said."

"There's no use discussing it. Jonathon's unsuitable."

"He just made one mistake, though. Where is the forgiveness in your heart?"

"He made many more than just one mistake, and he left his job suddenly and left Mark with no one on a day when Mark and Christina had an appointment." Florence shook her head. "The man *Gott* has for you would not do these kinds of things."

"But Isaac's got the job now. Joy told me that. Jonathon always felt Isaac should've had the job anyway because he's

Mark's *bruder*-in-law. He even told Mark to give him the job and he'd look for something else."

"We're not going to agree, Honor, so it's pointless talking about it. That just tells me he wasn't grateful for the job he had." Although she felt sorry for Honor, there was nothing more she could say. Time would heal her sister's heart. Florence walked back down the stairs and slipped some items into a basket for Carter—two apple pies, apple butter, chocolate cookies made from her grandmother's recipe and a large bottle of apple cider—and then announced she was going for a walk.

It was time to thank Carter properly. She'd been too short with him the other day and had brushed him off by refusing to see his renovations. He'd driven her around for hours in the daytime to look for Honor, and then he drove all the way to Connecticut and back in the night. It had been exhausting for her so she knew it would've been worse for him as the driver. It was Christmas time and she wanted him to know how much she'd appreciated his generosity.

As she approached his house, she knew he was home because she spotted his car.

She knocked on the door and when he took his time to answer, she walked to the window, looked in and smiled when she saw him playing on his computer with earphones in his ears. When she knocked loudly on the window, he looked up and then pulled off the earphones as he jumped up from the table.

He opened the door, smiling. "How's your sister?"

"Which one?"

"The one who was banished."

"Ah, she's good, I believe."

"You haven't talked with her?"

"I don't think she's talking to me. She thinks I was the one who sent her away. It was my stepmother's idea. Anyway, I think I told you that last time I was here."

"And the runaway sister?"

"She's doing okay. I'm hoping she'll forget about Jonathon." He slowly nodded and then she held out the basket. "These are for you. My way of saying thank you for all that you've done."

He took the basket from her and looked in it. "You have been busy. You did all this baking just for me?"

"Of course, especially just for you. Without you, I don't know what would've happened with Honor. We never would've found her in time."

"Things would've worked out. Now that you're here, come in and have a look at my renovations. I've been wanting to show them to someone."

"Sure. I'd like that." His words caused her to realize she'd never seen any of his friends there. No friends and no relatives—the man was a complete mystery.

He took the basket from her and led her through to the kitchen. She was impressed. A sparkling white and chrome kitchen had taken the place of the old one she remembered as a child.

"This is amazing. Truly beautiful."

He placed the basket down on the counter and took out all the contents. "Do you remember what it looked like?"

"Last time I was here the room was just a shell. I remember it as a child, but only vaguely. Before my father sold it he kept it ready for visitors, family and friends who came to stay."

He opened the cupboard and pulled out a little photo album. "This is what it looked like. I took these the day I moved in. The Graingers told me they never touched the place."

She picked up the album and flipped through it. Photos

always reminded her of her mother. More than anything she would've loved to know what she looked like. Her only memories were vague impressions of holding onto her mother's dress and her mother hoisting her onto her hip. People had told her she looked like her mother now that she was an adult, but her father had never mentioned her mother. By the time Florence was old enough to ask questions, he was married to Wilma.

She put the photo book back on the table after she'd looked through. "You've certainly done a lot of work."

He placed his hands on his hips and looked around. "I don't know what to do with the rest of it. I was going to paint the living room a neutral shade because it looks so outdated with the blue walls and the wood interior. I'll have to get rid of the wood."

"That's part of the charm, though. I think you'd destroy the place if you got rid of those features."

He smiled. "Do you think so?"

"I do."

"I'll show you the bathroom."

She followed him up the wooden staircase to a small bathroom. The ceiling was slanted.

"This was part of the old attic. It was remodeled at some stage, I guess when they went from outdoor to indoor plumbing." He pointed to the antique claw-foot bathtub. "I kept the same tub and had it sandblasted and re-enamelled."

"It's nice you've kept the lovely bathtub, and that's given the room so much appeal. It wouldn't be the same with a modern tub because the place is old."

He rubbed his neck. "I think you're right. But I couldn't live with the out-dated kitchen and I had to do something with this bathroom. I like a nice kitchen with all the mod cons."

She gave him a curious look.

"Modern conveniences."

"Oh. So, you like cooking?"

He chuckled. "I never cook."

She frowned wondering how he ate if he never cooked. "Never?"

"I don't cook, unless you count re-heating things, or thawing meals out and putting them in the microwave. That's the closest I've come to cooking. Or a frozen pizza in the oven."

"I see." She stared at him. From what she knew so far, he had no friends, no family and he couldn't cook. Add to that, he had plenty of free time, enough money even though he didn't have a job, and he was a self-confessed bad chess player. Maybe that's what she found appealing—the man was an enigma. When he smiled at her causing her heart to pitter-patter, she knew it was time to leave. "Anyway, Merry Christmas for tomorrow."

"Merry Christmas to you, Florence."

She turned away to walk down the stairs and when she was halfway down them, he said, "Are you going now?"

When she got to the bottom she turned around to see him on the last step. "Yes. We have guests for dinner. Well, one guest."

"A man?"

"That's right." She noticed the smile left his face as he ambled down the steps.

"Let me walk you to the fence. Wait, don't forget your basket." He got the empty basket from the kitchen and gave it back to her.

She giggled and then stopped abruptly when she sounded like one of her sisters, who often laughed at nothing at all. "Thanks."

He then opened the front door. "After you."

She walked past him and then stepped out into the chilly winter air.

As he walked beside her, he looked around. "I wonder if we'll get snow."

"I hope so. I love watching the snowflakes fall when I don't have to go out in it. If it snowed tomorrow it would be just perfect."

"You're not going to your church tomorrow for Christmas?"

"No. We don't do that. We celebrate at home with our friends and families."

He nodded.

"And, what will you do?"

"The same."

"You're having your family and friends come here when you don't cook? Are you going to microwave them a re-heated meal?"

He shook his head. "My friends are here already."

She frowned at him and he pointed to his cows. "Ah, yes, the cows you've adopted."

"I'll give them something special to eat—something Christmassy."

"I'm glad you won't be by yourself."

"A wise person once said that if you like your own company, you're never alone."

They'd reached the fence and he pulled up the wire for her and she bent down and slipped through to the other side still hanging onto her basket. When she straightened up, they held each other's gaze for a moment. There was something in those dark hazel eyes. She wanted to learn more about him—get to know him, but sadly that was out of the question. They could never be anything more than neighbors. "You're an interesting man, Carter." A complete riddle is what she meant. How did he get to this age and have no one with whom to spend Christmas day? He seemed nice and friendly, so surely, people didn't hate him. Was there something she wasn't seeing?

He was visibly shocked at her comment and that made her embarrassed. Like many of her comments, the words had rolled off her tongue before she'd thought about them. She hadn't meant it to sound like she was interested in him romantically. *Is that how he took it?*

As he stood there stunned, she said, "Bye. I have to go." She turned and walked away from him. This time, she was determined to stay away from him for good—at least for the rest of the year.

When Florence got home, she was ordered out of the kitchen by Joy, who had already told the others she was cooking the entire meal tonight since Isaac was coming. At least with Joy, Florence didn't foresee any problems.

Florence didn't mind in the least that someone was organizing the cooking and took the opportunity to have a much-needed nap.

Dinner that night, with Isaac as their guest, was pleasant especially since there was no talk of Jonathon.

CHAPTER 26

On Christmas morning, Florence got out of bed early, pushed her feet into her slippers and pulled on her robe. Then she hurried downstairs to tend to the fire. This was always the job of the first person to wake.

When she got to the bottom of the stairs, she saw the embers were still glowing keeping the house warm to some extent. Carefully, she lifted more kindling onto the embers until they caught alight, then she carefully arranged more logs.

She stood back and watched the flames grow higher and folded her arms around her middle.

This was the first year the girls weren't awake before her, and it was also the first Christmas they'd be without Mercy—and now, without Cherish. Tomorrow, the girls would be up way before dawn. The day after Christmas was called Second Christmas, traditionally their 'gift-giving day.' She walked past the wrapped presents in the corner of the room and moved quickly across the gray linoleum flooring to light the stove. After she rinsed and refilled the kettle and placed it over the flame, she stayed by the stove enjoying the warmth.

Things were always changing. She had a feeling that, come next Christmas, things would be different again. Hopefully Mercy would be back, and maybe even Cherish too, if she got over her silly notion of being in love with a much-older and unsuitable man that her older sister also liked. There was never a dull moment in a household with so many teenaged girls.

When the kettle boiled, Florence took hold of the coffee canister and shook out some grounds. She was used to measuring coffee that way and saved herself the chore of washing a spoon. Then she filled the plunger with the boiling water. She gave the container a little swirl and then waited a minute before she pushed the plunger down. Once she'd poured herself a cup, she sat at the table pleased to have this quiet time before the others woke.

The day was filled with visitors stopping by. Firstly, it was Levi Brunner and his daughter, Bliss. They brought with them a plum cake made by Bliss. Of course, *Mamm* invited them to stay for the midday meal. Florence could see what was happening. First the gift of a horse and now a casual visit on Christmas Day, with a cake. Levi Brunner was sweet on *Mamm.* Bliss was just happy to be with her friends, Favor and Hope.

Later, Ada and Samuel arrived along with Mark, Christina and Isaac. It was fairly crowded around the dinner table as they shared coffee, tea, cake and cookies.

~

Both Joy and Honor opened the door expecting to greet

Isaac. He'd gone home and was coming back again for the evening meal. He was to be the only guest for Christmas dinner.

The next thing Florence heard was Honor yelling out to her. Florence hurried over to her. "What is it?"

"It's a tree, and the note says, *Florence.* It's for you." Honor held it out to her.

Florence looked down at the small plant with the huge red ribbon and the tiny red envelope attached. Immediately, she recognized it as some kind of apple tree. She took it from Honor and sat down with it. She placed the tree in her lap and opened the note.

"So, what is it?" Hope rushed over.

"An apple tree." Florence could only laugh.

"Who's it from?"

"I'm trying to find that out." In her heart, Florence knew who it was from. She opened the note and read it to herself.

To my dear Florence,

I happened to come across this and thought you might like it. It's an already grafted Narragansett.

Your Secret Admirer

It was from Carter.

"Well? Who gave you that twig and spent so much time wrapping it up so fancy?" Joy asked with her hands firmly on her hips.

"No one. It's not a twig."

Favor grabbed the note and opened it. "A Secret Admirer!

Florence has a secret admirer. Florence is in love! Who could it be?"

Florence jumped up and snatched the note back. The girls stared at Florence in disbelief.

Hope said, "It's Levi Brunner. He gave us the horse."

"Nee, he likes *Mamm,"* Favor said. "He's way too old for Florence."

Isaac stood there looking embarrassed. Then, in the midst of their noisy speculations, friends of the girls arrived unexpectedly to visit, and the girls turned their attention to them. Florence took her gift and the handwritten note upstairs and hid them in her room.

Where ever did he find such a plant? She knew it must've come from another collector. She hurried back down the stairs to help with the dinner and there she saw that Ada and Samuel had arrived and so it was two more people at their table.

~

AFTER DINNER, Florence was washing up with Hope and they were talking about Honor and how she'd laughed and joined in with the conversation. It was almost like she was back to her old self. Florence hoped that in time she'd forget Jonathon Wilkes. It didn't help that his brother Stephen was married to Mercy. He'd never be out of her life completely.

Ada walked into the kitchen and said to Florence, "I have a surprise for you. I've been talking to Wilma and she asked me something."

"What?"

"I won't talk about it today. I'll tell you soon, though."

"What is it? You have to tell me now." Florence shook the water off her hands and wiped them on a towel. She hated not knowing things. "You must tell me."

Ada chuckled. "Wilma asked me if I knew someone suitable for you."

"Ach nee! I told her not to do that."

"At first I said I didn't. But then I remembered Ezekiel Troyer."

Hope put down the plate she'd been wiping dry. "And you think he'd be a good match for Florence?"

"Stop it, Hope," Florence said, not wanting to prolong this conversation.

"Well, she was right about Mercy and Stephen."

Ada looked with eagle eyes at Florence. "Will you meet him?"

Florence frowned. "Where's he from?"

"Not too far away."

"She'll meet him," Hope said.

"Now wait a minute."

"What harm could it do to meet the man? Especially when Wilma has already arranged for him to come to dinner here next week."

"She what?"

Ada nodded. "That's right he's coming here for dinner next week."

Florence blew out a deep breath.

"What's he like? What does he do?" Hope eagerly asked Ada.

"He's a pig farmer."

That wasn't something Florence wanted to hear. That conjured an image of a large sweaty man wearing large knee-high boots and too-large overalls and smelling of pigswill. Hope must've thought something similar because she burst out laughing.

"There's nothing wrong with pigs," said Ada.

"I know. Piglets are cute," Hope replied smiling. "I'd love

to have a pet piglet, but then they grow up and it wouldn't be so adorable."

Since he was coming for dinner, there was no way Florence could get out of it. "I'll meet him but only because he's already coming here. And please, Ada, don't do anything like this again. I don't care what *Mamm* tells you."

Ada nodded. "I didn't know. I thought you'd be pleased. That's why I was saving it as a surprise."

"Denke. I appreciate your efforts, but I did tell *Mamm* I wasn't interested in finding a man this way."

"Florence already has a secret admirer." Hope said. "He left a present at the door for her today."

Ada stared at Florence. "Is that so?"

Florence couldn't help but giggle. "It was just someone's idea of a joke. That's all." She didn't want rumors to start, so leaned over and whispered to Ada, "Just one of the girls having some fun."

CHAPTER 27

WHEN THE NIGHT was over and every one of the girls and Wilma were in bed, a weary Florence walked up the stairs. She pushed open her bedroom door and the light from the hallway lit her special apple tree. It seemed as though it was smiling back at her. Florence flicked on her light and turned off the gaslight in the hall. Then she sat at her window and looked out into the darkness in the direction of Carter's house.

Carter cared about her enough to find one of those apple trees she'd mentioned in passing. They weren't easy to come by and he would've gone to an awful lot of trouble finding a plant already grafted like that. He would've already had it when she was there yesterday. He'd planned all along to leave it on her doorstep for Christmas morning. For the first time in her life, she felt special.

Then an image of the pig farmer jumped into her mind. Was he the kind of man she would, or perhaps should, marry?

She closed her curtains and moved to the end of her bed.

Nothing could ever come from her attraction to the *Englischer.* He was off-limits. The best thing she could do was put Carter Braithwaite out of her mind altogether. They lived next-door, but they were worlds apart.

When she'd gotten changed, she climbed into her bed and once her head hit the pillow, she reviewed how much had happened in a few shorts weeks. Mercy had gotten married, Honor had tried to run away with Jonathon, and then Cherish had tried to run away. Now there were two girls missing from the house, since Cherish was staying with Aunt Dagmar and Mercy was married.

Florence's life was disappearing into the lives of those around her. She knew she had to make a change somewhere, someway, so she could have a life of her own. Otherwise, she'd live her life worried about her half-sisters.

Would Honor ever forget Jonathon? For that matter, would Cherish forget him? Or would both girls liking Jonathon cause a huge rift to develop in the family?

Running the orchard, the household and now the market stall was enough for any one person. She didn't need all of these other worries.

Falling asleep, she could feel time ticking by. Her life was moving so fast and she was getting older by the minute.

Weeks ago, she'd realized God was using Carter Braithwaite as a sign there was a good Amish man somewhere for her. Could the one she'd been waiting for be Ezekiel Troyer? Would the pig farmer be the answer to her having a life of her own?

HONOR HAD CRIED herself to sleep, and she woke up pining for Jonathon. Couldn't her family understand love? Surely *Mamm* knew what it was like to love because she'd loved *Dat.* She couldn't help being the age she was.

Since she'd been back she'd put on a brave face and had done the best she could to fit back in with the family, but she didn't want to be there. One thing she knew for a fact was that it made it worse for her that Cherish had a crush on Jonathon. It made it look like everyone was in love with him. The difference was that Cherish's love wasn't real and her's was.

Honor knew all she could do was pray. So she wouldn't fall asleep, she got out of her warm bed and kneeled down beside her bed and prayed that their love would find a way. She crawled back into her still-warm bed.

Soon, her sisters were squealing. It was Second Christmas and time to open the gifts. She changed into her day clothes, braided her hair, and after she placed her *kapp* on her head, she went downstairs. Her sisters were nowhere to be seen but her mother was in the living room talking to someone. Honor blinked twice, not believing her eyes. It was Jonathon.

He looked over and saw her and when he stood up, her mother pushed herself to her feet and walked over to her, smiling. "Jonathon has come here to explain everything. He's said he was sorry for running away with you."

Florence had walked down the stairs just a minute or so behind Honor and she did her own double take when she saw Jonathon. "What's going on?"

Mamm said, "Jonathon has come to say he's sorry. He's asked our forgiveness and I gave it. He's been here for nearly two hours and we've talked deeply and he's told me so much about himself."

Florence stood still, as stiff as a post.

Honor took another step forward. "Does that mean …?"

"You're still in trouble for doing what you did. You can't marry until you're eighteen, but if you still want to marry each other after that, we won't stand in your way."

This was what Honor had hoped for and she was thrilled Jonathon hadn't left her. He'd come back for her.

"You two can talk in the living room and we'll go to the kitchen." *Mamm* looked over at Florence. "Come along, Florence."

Florence was hugely upset. She'd done everything for the family and now on the important things *Mamm* completely overrode her—hadn't even asked for her opinion before she'd given 'their' forgiveness and blessing.

She kept her thoughts quiet, said nothing and walked into the kitchen with *Mamm* to join the rest of the girls.

Honor ran to Jonathon and threw her arms around him. "I'm so happy you came here."

"I had to. I couldn't be without you." He whispered into her ear, "We shouldn't get too close or I'll get kicked out."

She stepped away from him and then they sat down and he sat beside her holding both her hands in his. "I missed you so much I couldn't stay away. I thought your *mudder* would understand if I explained how we both felt. I've done so many things wrong, but there's always forgiveness."

"*Jah,* there is."

"We still have to wait a whole year."

"But we don't have to hide away anymore. You'll stay around here, *jah?"*

"I will. I've really learned some things. Some hard lessons. I should've stayed before, and talked to your mother and explained myself. It was impulsive to run away, and stupid. I'll get a job and I don't care where I stay as long as I can be close to you."

She giggled from sheer happiness.

"I want to be the best man I can be for you. I have nothing right now, no money, but I'll work hard and be a good provider. I'll have savings by the time we're married."

"I know you will and we'll get by." She put her head on his shoulder.

ONCE *MAMM* WAS in the kitchen, she peeped around the corner at Jonathon and Honor until Florence tugged at her sleeve.

"Looks like you've lost another *dochder* now. Is that what you wanted? To have her marry so young?" Florence was annoyed and it was hard to hide it.

"I said they'd have to wait until she's eighteen." *Mamm's* eyes grew wide. "Florence, I can't stop them. Not when she's this age. I haven't lost her, but I know I'd lose her if I told them they couldn't marry."

Florence placed her hands on her hips thinking about Cherish. "That also means that Cherish will have to stay at Aunt Dagmar's for longer or she'd surely get in their way while they're courting."

"You're right. That would be best. I hope Cherish is okay staying there."

"The question is how Aunt Dagmar is coping with Cherish." Florence and *Mamm* shared a giggle. Florence could see what a hard situation *Mamm* was in. "Did Jonathon tell you why I'm against him?"

"Jah, he told me what he did and he said he was sorry. Both his *bruder* and Mercy forgave him."

"He's family now so they kind of had to."

"He said he couldn't change his past and all the dumb things he'd done, but he'd learn from all his mistakes and not repeat them. I believe him. He said he'd talk to you too."

Florence nodded, hoping Jonathon meant every word. Words were easy, actions were harder.

While Florence's sisters were busy making breakfast,

chattering away about when they'd open their presents, Honor walked into the kitchen. "Florence, will you talk with Jonathon?"

"He wants to talk to me?"

"*Jah.* I'll stay in the kitchen."

Florence wasn't in the mood. She looked at *Mamm* who gave her an encouraging nod. She walked out to see Jonathon sitting down and then he jumped to his feet as she approached. "I'm sorry about everything, Florence."

She sat down opposite and he sat down too. Before she could say anything, he said, "I know you don't like me, but—"

"If you want me to be frank with you, I liked you when I first met you—up until I started to see a side of you I didn't like. Then when you tricked Mercy, I didn't want you anywhere near any of my sisters."

"I'm deeply sorry about that and I've said I'm sorry already. I didn't mean it to happen how it turned out."

"I know that, but it was still designed to drive a wedge between the two of them."

He hung his head. "I was jealous of Stephen." He looked up at her. "All the girls have always liked him more than me. Then when he came here and I saw the same thing happen, I was more annoyed than ever. It was awful of me to do what I did, I can see that now."

"That's good."

"I can't change what I've done. People can only learn from their mistakes, they can't un-make them, and I've certainly learned from mine. I no longer want to be the trickster, or the manipulator. I just want to live a Godly life with Honor as my *fraa.* I'll wait as long as I have to or do whatever I have to do to prove to you all that I'm a good person."

"Well, Honor certainly believes that and I'd hate for her to be disappointed."

"She won't be. And, Honor just told me that Cherish tried running away, and I can sincerely say I never gave her any encouragement."

"I know. I believe that."

He gave a sigh of relief. "What about you, though? It seems you're acting like the girls' mother, when you're only a girl yourself. An older girl, but still a girl and your looks haven't faded completely."

Florence stared at him. "I'm none of your concern."

"I didn't mean to be offensive. I just meant that I would've thought you might have wanted to get out more and meet people or something. Instead of worrying about your sisters."

"Just when I was starting to find forgiveness in my heart you go and ruin it."

He stared at her, a worried expression crossing his face, and then smiled when he saw that she was smiling. "You had me concerned there for a minute. I've got this problem that I don't think too hard before I open my big mouth."

"That's one thing you and I have in common, then."

"I also want to say that I know I used to act on impulse, but now I've got Honor to consider. I'm working on changing my ways and my whole personality. I'm going to be that good and responsible man she deserves."

Florence knew in her heart that he was genuinely trying. "I'm glad we talked."

"I mean every word I said."

"I hope so." She stood up. "I'll help in the kitchen and send Honor back out. I'm sure you two have loads to talk about."

"We do."

"And…" She wagged a finger at him. "No running away again."

"No way!"

She smiled at him, and then walked to the kitchen.

Honor's face was the first she saw. "You can go back to speak with him."

"How did it go?"

"Good. He told me a few things and I believe he's genuine."

Honor's eyes sparkled and she hurried out of the kitchen.

Mamm looped her arm through Florence's. *"Denke,* Florence. Your approval means everything."

"It's my reserved approval. I'll see how he does over the next few months."

"Ada and I have a surprise for you."

Florence grimaced before she could stop herself. "The pig farmer?" Neither could she prevent the image of the man coming into her mind.

"Jah. She told you already?"

Florence sank into a chair. "She did."

"It's your turn for something nice to happen for you." *Mamm* patted her on her shoulder.

Florence hoped that it was true. She turned away, closed her eyes and superimposed Carter's face over the image she held of the Amish pig farmer. It didn't quite fit. Even though she knew little about Carter, there was something about him that made her want to learn more.

Bishop Paul's words echoed in her mind. She had to stay on the narrow way—the narrow path. The more time she spent with Carter, the closer she'd get to the edge of that path. The Amish life was the only one she'd known and nothing and no one would cause her to leave. Being around Carter too much put her at risk of doing just that. He was a temptation and, like all temptations, he had to be avoided.

Florence turned around, looked at her mother and said the only thing a good Amish daughter could say. "When, exactly, do I meet this pig farmer?"

"Next week. I think he's arriving midweek. Did I tell you he's interested in apple trees?"

Florence could hardly believe her ears. "Why didn't you say that in the first place?"

"Whoops. That was Ada's special part of the surprise." Wilma put her hand over her mouth and giggled.

Someone with a common interest? He mightn't be too bad.

She wouldn't have long to wait to find out since he was coming to dinner next week.

JONATHON STAYED with the family for breakfast and then left to find himself accommodation. He'd said he didn't think he'd be welcome back at Mark's and Christina's, but since he was determined to mend his ways, he'd assured them his first stop would be their place to offer his apologies for letting them down.

THAT NIGHT, Florence walked into Honor's bedroom as Honor was getting into bed.

"Denke, schweschder, for accepting Jonathon."

She sat down on the end of Honor's bed while Honor slipped between the sheets. "He seemed sincere and I'm prepared to give him a second chance."

"I know, and I appreciate it."

Florence thought about her friend, Liza. She'd said she was in love with Simon and then the love soured after marriage. *Gott* had blessed them with rekindled love when their son was born, but Florence knew the discord could just as easily have gone on. "Take this next year to get to know him thoroughly. The good and the bad. You could be married for sixty years or even more and you have to make sure he's truly the right one for you."

"He is."

Florence shook her head. "With that attitude, you could find yourself making a mistake. I want you to have in your mind 'is he?' rather than 'he is.' Do you understand the difference?"

HONOR STARED at Florence's face. Her older sister's eyes were bloodshot and her skin was pale. Lines were forming around the edges of her eyes. She was getting old. "I do, but I love him."

When Honor giggled, Florence rolled her eyes. "What's the use?"

"Just be happy for me."

"I'm fearful that you'll marry him and then realize he's not who you thought he'd be."

"That won't happen because you and *Mamm* are forcing us to wait a whole year."

Florence nodded. "That's good."

Honor fluffed up the pillows behind her and then scooted to sit with them behind her back. "Have you ever been in love?"

Florence took a deep breath. "I've liked a couple of men in the past, but nothing came of it. I didn't get close enough to love them."

"Do you even want to marry?"

"*Jah*, I do."

Honor found that hard to believe. "You do?"

"*Jah.* Why do you say it like that?"

"It's just that I can't picture you with anyone."

Florence nodded. "Me neither, I'm sad to say."

"He'd have to be someone really special."

"*Mamm* and Ada think they have such a man and he's

coming to dinner next week. He's a pig farmer and they think … well, Ada thinks we'd be a match."

"A pig farmer? Hope told me that but I thought she was joking." Honor put her hand to her mouth and giggled. "I suppose someone has to farm pigs."

"He might be okay. He might be my perfect match."

"I hope so, for your sake. But then, what would we all do without you? And what about the orchard? It can't run without you."

"I wouldn't leave the orchard."

"But how—?"

Florence shook her head. "That's way too far ahead, and it might never happen. Right now, I'm glad you're going to take what I've said into account."

"I'll remember. 'Is he,' rather than 'he is,' right?"

"*Jah.* You're only young yet, and there are lots of choices out there for you."

"Choices?"

"Lots of men."

Honor was a little annoyed with Florence for not understanding that Jonathon was the man she'd chosen. "I know you're only saying that because you're worried, but Jonathon is good. He's the man I love, and we know his family. When Mercy married Stephen, no one was so worried about that and they're brothers."

"Just pray about it and then after a year if you still want to marry him I'll be happy for you."

"Just be happy now, anyway."

Florence giggled. "Okay. I'll be happy."

"And stop looking for things to be worried about. In life, there are always problems, but we can't go around being gloomy."

"That's true."

"We all have to make our own decisions in life and all of us aren't going to make the decisions you'd make because we're not you."

Florence smiled, but still, the worry never left her eyes. "You're wise sometimes for someone so young."

"Denke. I try."

Florence leaned forward and kissed Honor's forehead. *"Gut nacht."*

"Gut nacht."

When Florence was gone, Honor flicked off the light on her nightstand and lowered herself further into bed. Everything had turned around to suit her. Jonathon had loved her so much that he'd come back and faced her mother and Florence. That had taken great courage.

I'm sure they still doubt him, but I don't. Not one little bit.

Florence walked into her own bedroom feeling more at ease with the idea of Honor and Jonathon. Sure, he'd made mistakes, but he said he was willing to learn from them and she believed him to be sincere.

As she crawled into bed, she wondered why love had come so easily for others while for her it was just some far-off hazy notion. She wanted to love someone and be loved in return. Not just any man would do. She didn't want to marry for the sake of marrying. What she wanted was to be loved with deep abiding and unconditional love. That love though, had to come with one proviso. She had to be able to continue with the orchard because she couldn't imagine a life without her apple trees. It seemed implausible, but she knew that with God all things were possible. He'd make a way where there was no way.

With her mouth curving into a smile, the prayer on Florence's lips that night was to find such a love.

~

I HOPE you enjoyed reading Amish Honor.
Samantha Price

ALSO BY SAMANTHA PRICE:

AMISH MAIDS TRILOGY

Book 1 His Amish Nanny

Book 2 The Amish Maid's Sweetheart

Book 3 The Amish Deacon's Daughter

AMISH MISFTIS

Book 1 The Amish Girl Who Never Belonged

Book 2 The Amish Spinster

Book 3 The Amish Bishop's Daughter

Book 4 The Amish Single Mother

Book 5 The Temporary Amish Nanny

Book 6 Jeremiah's Daughter

Book 7 My Brother's Keeper

SEVEN AMISH BACHELORS

Book 1 The Amish Bachelor

Book 2 His Amish Romance

Book 3 Joshua's Choice

Book 4 Forbidden Amish Romance

Book 5 The Quiet Amish Bachelor

Book 6 The Determined Amish Bachelor

Book 7 Amish Bachelor's Secret

EXPECTANT AMISH WIDOWS

Book 1 Amish Widow's Hope

Book 2 The Pregnant Amish Widow

Book 3 Amish Widow's Faith

Book 4 Their Son's Amish Baby

Book 5 Amish Widow's Proposal

Book 6 The Pregnant Amish Nanny

Book 7 A Pregnant Widow's Amish Vacation

Book 8 The Amish Firefighter's Widow

Book 9 Amish Widow's Secret

Book 10 The Middle-Aged Amish Widow

Book 11 Amish Widow's Escape

Book 12 Amish Widow's Christmas

Book 13 Amish Widow's New Hope

Book 14 Amish Widow's Story

Book 15 Amish Widow's Decision

Book 16 Amish Widow's Trust

Book 17 The Amish Potato Farmer's Widow

Book 18 Amish Widow's Tears

Stand-Alone Christmas novel:

In Time For An Amish Christmas

For a full list of Samantha Price's books visit:

www.SamanthaPriceAuthor.com

ABOUT SAMANTHA PRICE

Samantha Price wrote stories from a young age, but it wasn't until later in life that she took up writing full time. Formally an artist, she exchanged her paintbrush for the computer and, many best-selling book series later, has never looked back.

Samantha is happiest on her computer lost in the world of her characters. She is best known for the *Ettie Smith Amish Mysteries* series and the *Expectant Amish Widows* series.

To learn more about Samantha Price and her books visit:
www.SamanthaPriceAuthor.com

~

Samantha Price loves to hear from her readers. Connect with her at:

samanthaprice333@gmail.com
www.facebook.com/SamanthaPriceAuthor
Follow Samantha Price on BookBub
Twitter @ AmishRomance

Made in the USA
Columbia, SC
23 April 2019